In grateful to Yoko

GHOST
NOTE
. . .

Joan,
  I'm grateful to Yaddo
that our paths finally
crossed..

Lana

November 1992

GHOST NOTE

Zena Collier

GROVE WEIDENFELD

New York

Published by Grove Weidenfeld
A division of Grove Press, Inc.
841 Broadway
New York, New York 10003-4793

Published in Canada by General Publishing Company, Ltd.

TROUBLE IS A MAN words and music by Alec Wilder. Copyright 1944
(renewed) Ludlow Music, Inc., New York. All rights for the USA
controlled by Ludlow Music, Inc. All rights for territories of the
world excluding USA controlled by Regent Music Corp. All rights
reserved. Reprinted by permission.

ON THE SUNNY SIDE OF THE STREET by Dorothy Fields and Jimmy McHugh
copyright 1930 Shapiro, Bernstein & Co., Inc., New York, and
The Songwriter's Guild, New York. Copyright renewed.
Used by permission.

RED SAILS IN THE SUNSET by Jimmy Kennedy and Hugh Williams
copyright 1935 Shapiro, Bernstein & Co., Inc., New York. Copyright
renewed. Used by permission.

LIBRARY OF CONGRESS CATALOGING-IN-PUBLICATION DATA
Collier, Zena, 1926–
    Ghost note / Zena Collier.—1st ed.
        p.   cm.
    ISBN 0-8021-1513-6 (acid-free paper)
    I. Title.
PR6069.H75G46   1992
823'.914—dc20   91-41046
                                                            CIP

Manufactured in the United States of America

Printed on acid-free paper

Designed by Kathryn Parise

First Edition 1992

10 9 8 7 6 5 4 3 2 1

For Paul

I am deeply grateful to the MacDowell Colony
and the Virginia Center for the Creative Arts,
where much of this book was written.

GHOST

NOTE

• • •

PROLOGUE

• • •

He was a small, spare man, all the color gone from him; his pale, sloping eyes might once have been blue, his thin, limp hair might once have been sandy. Because he was trim, you might take him, at first glance, for a man of sixty. In fact, he had just turned seventy.

Now, standing by the car while the numbers on the gasoline pump flicked rapidly upward, he stretched his arms back and forth in an effort to ease the aching muscles of his shoulders.

"How far from the Shelburne exit to the city?"

"Not far." The attendant closed the hood with a clang. "Keep left at Burnett—unless you want the college—?"

"No."

"Keep left at Burnett, then, and you'll make it in fifteen minutes. Maybe beat the rain." He glanced upward. "Boy, it's going to be a dilly!"

He paid for the gas, got back in the car, and drove off, yawning. He had been driving all morning along the highway, watching the shifting cloud-filled sky spread like a canopy over the countryside and the small towns with Dutch names and the medium-sized manufacturing cities. He had forgotten these skies, these upstate skies, in the years he'd been gone.

But an hour earlier, there had been a change; the day had turned eerie, half the sky lit with October sunshine, the other half stained a menacing purple-black. The stain had spread, until now, at two o'clock, a premature dusk seemed to have fallen. He frowned as a distant rumble sounded. He would have preferred to arrive in a peaceable calm; it would help, somehow, if the time of his coming were as undramatic as possible. Perhaps, though, he could still beat the storm. At least it was not yet raining.

He drove faster, passing industrial parks, shopping malls, apartment complexes. Twice he had to detour because of construction. A billboard flashed WELCOME TO SHELBURNE, BUILDING FOR A BETTER TOMORROW. PARDON OUR DUST. This burgeoning city in western New York, population half a million souls, still prospered, apparently.

The sky grew darker still as he left the highway and crossed a bridge over the river that flowed through the center of town. Driving across, he gazed at the altered skyline, now completely dominated by skyscrapers that dwarfed the old factories and the crumbling flour mills that still lined the river.

When he reached the other side, he at once became embroiled in a grid of no-left-turns, one-way streets, and pedestrian malls in a downtown section he hardly recognized. Drivers shouted at him as he backed and turned, a policeman directed him brusquely, and finally he extricated himself and, driving steadily, left all that behind him.

Soon he arrived in one of the older residential neighborhoods on the east side of town. The avenues here were broad and tree-lined, the houses well maintained despite signs of change. Some of the larger houses on Delevan Road had been converted to apartments. A sign, RICHARD'S TABLE, hung in the stained glass window of a freshly painted Victorian house on Fairwell Avenue. He drove along Fairwell to Cooley, down Cooley to Jessamine. As he ap-

proached the end of Jessamine, he began to slow. Finally he drew
to a stop before the house on the corner.

He pulled over to the curb, got out, and stood looking at the
house. It was a large frame house, painted dark green. Half a dozen
steps carpeted in sisal led up to the porch that ran across the front.
At the upstairs windows, shades were drawn, giving the house an
inhospitable look, which seemed further justified by the realtor's
announcement, SOLD, prominently displayed on the lawn. His eyes
lingered on the sign.

As though on cue, a shocking brilliance flickered, an explosion
rent the air, followed by sonorous rumbling. *Donner und Blitzen*,
noises off, all effects ready for the Confrontation Scene, he
thought wryly.

A man hurrying by on the other side of the street called,
"What number you looking for?"

The heavens opened.

"Oh—thanks," he called back, and hurried through the
downpour toward the porch steps. "I know where I am."

CHAPTER
1 . . .

An hour before the rain started, two women sat in the kitchen at the rear of the house. One lit a cigarette. The other studied a list. "Do you want the everyday dishes, Diane, or should they go in the sale?"

"Put them in the sale. I'd just like the teapot. The brown one."

"What about the good set?"

"I keep telling you, Lois, I've no room for anything else. My apartment's finite, after all." Diane repressed a sigh. "Anyway, my life-style doesn't exactly encompass fine china. I prefer stuff I can throw in the dishwasher."

"You never know. You might change your life-style someday." Her tone was dry.

"Perhaps. Just now, I don't even know where I'd put it."

"All right. But remember it's in my attic if you change your mind."

"I—" Diane broke off. "Yes, I will want it later, I'm sure. I appreciate your keeping it for me." She touched her sister's arm. "Don't mind me, Lo. I think it's delayed reaction."

"I know. Me, too."

For a moment the silence between them grew companionable. "Strange," Diane said. "I still can't get used to the idea. I keep thinking I'll look up and see her coming in. Or working here"— she touched the surface of the wooden table, which was scored with knife marks and many scrubbings—"getting an order ready, Ella helping."

Lois nodded. "After all, it's been barely a month." She stood. "Would you like some tea?"

Diane nodded absently. Only a month since their mother's death, true, but it was close to three months since she had first been taken ill. Coming in with a bag of groceries, she had suddenly crumpled to the floor right here in the kitchen, her workroom, where bowls and skillets hung on the walls and saucepans dangled from an overhead rack that traversed the room so that, working at the table or the counter or the large commercial range, she had only to reach up to choose the one she wanted, as though picking a plum from a tree. Large covered bins containing rice, onions, and potatoes stood in a corner; keeping them filled had been Ella's job. For the first time in Diane's memory, these would not be replenished when they were empty.

When Fay collapsed, Ella had telephoned Lois, screaming, "Come quick! Mother fell!" It turned out to be a massive cerebral hemorrhage. The prognosis was poor: the end could come at any time, or she might linger on for weeks. When Lois called Diane in New York City, Diane took the next plane out. She had been staying here in the house with Ella since then.

Lois brought mugs of tea to the table. "Is there lemon?"

"Bottom shelf."

Diane watched as Lois squeezed lemon in her tea. In that good silk blouse, wool skirt, and pearls, Lois looked far too well dressed for the job they were doing now, going through all the rooms, choosing and marking what would be taken, what would be sold or given away. But Lois always took exceptional care with her appearance—and with herself, for that matter. She always had.

Even as a child, she had never splashed through puddles. "You'll ruin your shoes!" she had cried at Diane and Ella. She had never raced up the stairs two at a time or slid down the banister. "Diane, you'll break your neck! I *told* you!" she cried unhelpfully when Diane, aged ten, tripped and took a swan dive down the basement stairs. She had always turned down invitations to go skating or sledding: "It's so messy out there." "It's not, it's not! You're an old grandma, that's what you are!" Diane taunted.

Lately it had struck Diane that Lois, not yet forty, seemed in temperament older than their mother had been. In appearance, she was handsome. Her dark hair was cut strictly short and straight, which made her look severe, but her lips had a decidedly sensual curve. And though her body's fullness was a little too heavy for fashion, it suggested a voluptuous richness hidden under those slightly matronly clothes. Did she ever—had she ever—let herself go with someone other than Gordon? Somehow, Diane couldn't picture it—not even with Gordon, for that matter. After all, sex was an untidy procedure; it was difficult to imagine Lois thus engaged, except in the most sedate fashion, no heavy breathing.

Lois took spoons from a drawer. "How dark it's grown. There must be a storm on the way." She flicked the light switch, and the room jumped into harsh relief. Above the refrigerator, the second hand on the large round wall clock crept soundlessly forward.

"What time did that man say he'd be coming?"

"What man?" Diane asked.

"The one who called about the piano."

"Three, three-thirty."

"I hope the weather doesn't put him off. Did he sound seriously interested?"

"I think so." Diane stirred her tea thoughtfully. "I'll be sad to see the piano go. It was so much part of Mother."

Before her marriage and for a while afterward, Fay had been a piano teacher. Later she had given up teaching and started the catering business with which she had supported them, but she had still played. As a child Diane had loved hearing her; whenever she'd brought friends home from school, she had urged Fay to the piano, where Fay would oblige with a Strauss waltz or a Schumann arabesque, or show tunes, folk songs. Fay had always hoped that one of her daughters would take up a musical career of some kind. Diane had no musical ability of any sort, and nothing, of course, could be expected of Ella. But Lois had seemed a likely prospect. She was only an adequate pianist, but she had a surprisingly sweet and true contralto, which earned her leading roles in high school musicals. As Ado Annie or Marian the librarian, she delivered her spoken lines rather flatly, but she never failed to give an accurate and melodic rendition of the songs. Fay always flushed with pleasure as the audience in the high school auditorium applauded heartily. But when she urged Lois to get training and go on to music school, Lois balked.

"I don't know if that's what I want."

"But if you do—"

"I don't have to decide right now, do I? I'm only a junior."

"Lois—"

"It's *my* life! I'll do what I want!"

Ultimately she had gone not to the conservatory that Fay had in mind but to the university that stood on the banks of the river that divided Shelburne. She majored in history. And right after graduation she married her American history professor, a tall man with hooded eyes and a small mustache, a widower nineteen years her senior.

●   ●   ●

"Do *you* want the piano?" Lois asked. "Well, then, what's the point of keeping it? I can store a lot in my attic and basement, but a grand piano's another matter. We'd have to pay to store it. It would only deteriorate. . . ."

Everything she said made sense, Diane thought. Certainly a piano was the last thing Ella needed. And Lois and Gordon already owned a piano.

"Perhaps Amy, someday—"

"Amy plays flute, not piano. Anyway, by the time she's ready for it—even if she wanted it—it wouldn't be worth having if it hadn't been used."

There was certainly no point in suggesting Ned. At the thought of Ned, she felt a rush of compassion. Poor Lois. No wonder she seemed so edgy these days. Let the piano go, then. Lois's practicality might seem ruthless at times, but some kinds of difficulties couldn't be solved without it.

Just then a slight but regular thumping sound began above their heads.

Lois sighed. "I wish she wouldn't do that."

"What harm does it do?"

"That isn't the point. It's creepy, the way she incarcerates herself up there."

Ever since Fay's death, Ella had established herself in Fay's bedroom. She spent most of her time there, swaying back and forth in the rocking chair, arms wrapped about herself as though to supply a comfort no one else could provide. Or she would sit on the floor with her back against the bed, lank hair falling around her gaunt face, long legs splayed, like a Raggedy Ann doll. At these times she seemed more than ever childlike, despite her thirty-two years.

"We ought to insist she leave that room."

"She comes down for meals."

"You know what I mean," Lois said, irritably. "She's going to have to leave soon, like it or not—not just the room but the house. We should start getting her used to the idea."

"Let her take it slowly. She's grieving, Lo."

"She's not the only one."

"It's worse for her, though. You and I went off to lives of our own, but she was with Mother all the time."

"This will only make it harder for her in the long run." Lois went to the stove and refilled her cup. "I know what you're thinking—that I'm hardhearted, hardheaded, putting the house on the market right away, wanting Ella to face up to changes. But facts are facts. The house is old and needs constant maintenance. And winter's coming, with heat bills. It would have been harder to sell in the winter. All very well for *you*, you flit in and out, you have none of—"

"In all fairness, Lois, I've been here ever since Mother got sick."

"But you don't live here, you don't have any of the responsibility—"

"That's not so! Don't you think I feel—"

"You might feel it, but you don't have to *do* anything. I'm the one everything falls on."

"But—"

Even while she protested, Diane felt a tiny, secret thrill of guilt, knowing there was a certain amount of truth in her sister's words. The fact that she didn't live here automatically freed her from much of the burden. And yes, she did feel that decisions were being made too quickly, even though they might be the right decisions.

Life had taken on the aspect of a speeded-up movie after Fay had become ill. Totally paralyzed, except for one eye. That eye had seemed to focus on them pleadingly, while the other remained fixed in its upward stare. It had been hard to realize this was Fay—sturdy, vigorous Fay, with her lined, rosy face, robust laugh, volatile temper. Fay, who had never been sick with anything worse than the flu and who liked to say she was strong as a horse. And at sixty-three she was—or had seemed to be.

Not only physically. It had taken a good deal of strength, physical and otherwise, to do what she'd done—running a business, bringing up and supporting three children on her own.

Especially when one of those children was Ella. Only in fairly recent years had Diane come to realize how heavy a burden that must have been, quite apart from what Fay must have suffered on her own account, her husband walking out all those years ago. But Fay never spoke of that. Hadn't mentioned so much as the name of that absent figure for many years.

Charles.

There had been no mention of him, no letters or photographs, among Fay's effects—only a copy of the divorce decree, granted on grounds of desertion. For evidence of the fact that he had actually existed, Diane, Lois, and Ella had only themselves. They had never heard from him. Where he might be, what he might be doing were unknown. He could be anywhere in the world, or out of it. Chances were about even, she supposed. Who could tell how life had treated him, to what vicissitudes—accidents, illness, and other assorted trials—he might have fallen prey in all this time?

Often, as she'd grown into adolescence, she had studied herself in the mirror, wondering. With her slight build, pale, fair coloring, and thin, sharp nose, she certainly didn't look like her mother. Fay's hair had been dark before it began to gray; Fay had heavier features and a solid frame, broad shoulders, a deep bosom, large wrists and hands. It was Lois and Fay who, from their appearances, were obviously mother and daughter.

Since she didn't resemble her mother, Diane supposed it must be Charles she resembled. Charles. Father. As a child she had longed to know. But the only person who could have told her was Fay, and both Diane and Lois had always understood implicitly that the subject of Charles was off-limits. All they knew was that, like their mother, he was—had been—a pianist. He'd taught piano and theory at the Adler School in Shelburne. To supplement his income, he had also played on weekends for parties, dances, weddings—music for dancing.

But how he looked or sounded, what he thought, believed, felt, Diane had no notion at all; she had been less than two years old when he left. And Ella couldn't possibly remember him, for she'd been born after his departure. Only Lois, who was six years old when he went, could feasibly have even the faintest recollection of him.

Years back Diane had pressed her for any details she could recall, but Lois had had very little to offer. "I vaguely remember him playing the piano, that's all. I don't remember him or what he looked like doing it, just the sound."

"Are you sure that wasn't Mother?"

"No, it was his kind of music. Jazz. Something fast and rhythmic. I remember trying to dance to it, jumping up and down. Anyway, why would I want to remember him? After what he did to Mother? To us? Leaving us to starve, for all he cared."

"I'm curious, that's all. Don't you ever wonder—"

"I don't wonder. I *hope*," Lois said. "I hope very much that he got what he deserved. Though I doubt it. That's not the way life works, is it?"

•   •   •

"Lois, you misunderstood," Diane said. "I'm not being critical. I understand all the difficulties. I agree it made sense to put the house up for sale. And there's nothing to do but sell the piano. All I'm saying is, we should try to make the transition as gradual as possible for Ella."

Lois seemed somewhat mollified. "Well, as gradual as we can, I suppose, considering the Mahacheks want possession December tenth." One hand plucked absently at her pearls. "I know you have to get back to New York, but can I count on you to stay long enough to help decide what ought to be done about Ella? And help get her settled, wherever?"

"Of course."

Suddenly Lois gave one of the infrequent full smiles that lightened and changed her face. In that moment she looked so much like Fay that Diane felt both startled and saddened. She thought, It's not fair. For Lois, who in that moment smiled their mother's smile exactly, and who had always been a far more dutiful daughter than Diane, had never really gotten along with Fay. And Diane, who hadn't seen a great deal of Fay in recent years, had nevertheless—she knew—received the greater share of Fay's affection. It wasn't just, it wasn't right, but there it was. Facts, as Lois would say, were facts.

·   ·   ·

The thing was, Fay had never really forgiven Lois for getting married as and when she did.

"I've nothing personal against Gordon," she'd said when Lois had first announced her plans. "But he's almost twice your age. And you're barely twenty, at the very beginning of—"

"How old were *you*?" Lois retorted.

Diane, fifteen, held her breath, listening.

"Oh, yes!" Fay cried, flaring. "And you see how that turned out!"

"This is different! Gordon's settled and decent and honorable! Gordon loves me! Gordon would never—"

"Gordon-Gordon-Gordon-Gordon," Ella crooned raucously, as though trying out the sound. She snickered.

Lois turned scarlet. "Shut up!"

"She's only—"

"I'm sick to death of her nauseating nonsense!" She started out of the room, then paused to hurl back a warning. "You and Diane had better see she behaves herself at the wedding! I don't want to be disgraced in front of everybody!"

But the next day Lois had been exceptionally kind to Ella, as though to make up. She washed and set Ella's hair and tried to style it, that straight, mousy hair which always resisted attempts at waves or a flattering fullness. She sat with Ella and watched some of the television shows Ella loved.

And Diane heard her apologize to Fay.

"I didn't mean—I was only trying to make you see that Gordon's—"

"That's all right, pet, I understand." Fay looked up from her desk, where she sat paying bills. Her face softened. "I didn't mean to imply there's anything wrong with Gordon."

"I love Gordon," Lois said earnestly. "He makes me feel so— safe. And I want my own home, and children, and—to be *normal*, that's all."

Fay's expression changed. "You don't feel you are right now?"

"Oh, Mother! Don't make a federal case out of it! Is there something wrong with wanting to be happy?"

Fay looked at the pen she was holding, as though wondering how it had got there. She laid it down. "Of course not. That's all I want—for you to be happy." She smiled. "All right. It's settled. Let's plan. . . ." Her tone became businesslike, the kind of tone she used with clients. "The wedding. What date are you thinking of?"

•   •   •

The reception was held at the house. Fay, Diane, and Ella made all the food, including a three-tier wedding cake that was topped, at Lois's request, with a tiny bride and groom. The miniature frock-coated figure did in fact look a little like Gordon, Diane thought; it was true the figure on the cake looked short and square, whereas Gordon was tall and thin, but there was something about the figure's stance and the eyes facing strictly front and center. . . . What on earth did Lois see in him? Safety. What did that mean? It made marriage sound like something to do with traffic. Was it money? For Gordon wasn't dependent on his income as a teacher; he came from a rather affluent background.

On the night after the wedding, Diane was awakened in the small hours by a sound she couldn't at first identify. It was three o'clock. A welcome stirring of air came through the window, which stood open to the warm summer night. She lay still, listening. The sound came from downstairs. It couldn't be Ella, for just then she heard Ella turning over in bed in the room across the hall.

She got out of bed and went downstairs.

It was Fay in the kitchen. She wore only her nightgown, with her butcher-style apron over it. Beneath the fabric, her breasts moved cumbrously as she went back and forth between the stove and the table. She had pinned her hair back tightly, as she always did when she worked. Her face and neck were filmed with sweat.

"Mother—what are you doing?"

"Getting the Larsen order ready." The hand holding the knife moved lightning-fast as she trimmed the edges of phyllo leaves.

"It's the middle of the night!"

"I couldn't sleep. Might as well get something done." Her tone was grim.

Diane said cautiously, "Don't you feel well?"

"I feel fine. Why not?" She picked up the pastry brush and dipped it in melted butter. "If you want to be useful, melt some more butter." Too vigorously, she began to brush butter on the paper-thin dough. The brush ripped through the delicate pastry. She hurled the brush down. "What a waste!"

"We can fix—"

"I mean Lois! Cutting off her life before it began!"

"But she wants—"

"Wants! She's too young to know what she wants!" Fay pounded her hand so hard on the table that flour jumped out of the holes in the sifter. Suddenly she strode over to Diane and seized her by the arms. "Don't *you* make the same mistake!"

"Mother!" Diane squirmed. "You're hurting me! Let go!"

Fay shook her. "Listen to what I'm saying!"

"I'm listening!"

"You're not!"

"Anyway, I don't know what you're making such a fuss about, I'm only—"

"Time goes fast, Diane."

"Let *go!*" She finally managed to wrench free. "Don't worry,
I'm not getting married. Even if I did, it wouldn't be for years and
years. Anyway, I told you—I'm going to be a poet."

Fay went back to the table and picked up the brush.
"Whatever"—she shook the brush at Diane for emphasis—"don't
invest all of yourself in a man! You'll be sorry!"

●   ●   ●

All these years later Diane could still feel that steely grip, could
still see Fay's eyes bearing into her as though to persuade by the
force of intensity.

"I'm sorry, Lois. You said—?"

"I said as long as we're on the subject, this is probably as good a
time as any to discuss what we ought to do about Ella."

"All right." Diane braced herself mentally for what she knew
was coming.

Lois crossed her arms and leaned back against the refrigerator.
"Would you take her to live with you?"

"In New York? How could I?"

"Why not? You're not working at a nine-to-five job, after all."

Diane flushed with annoyance. "Nine-to-five or not, I don't
spend my days lounging in a hammock. And I do need privacy and
no interruptions while I work. And much of the time I'm out
interviewing or doing research. And what about when I travel?"

"You'd have to get someone to stay with her."

"And when I'm writing at home? My place is tiny. We'd be on
top of each other."

"You'd have to get a bigger place. And you'd have to enforce
some rules. Ella would have to understand that she couldn't
interrupt—"

"It simply can't be done, Lois. Not in my present circumstances." In the pause that followed, she began to light another
cigarette.

"I wish you wouldn't do that," Lois said. "The smoke really bothers me."

Diane put away the cigarette. "In any case, doesn't it make more sense for her to stay in Shelburne, in what is at least a familiar environment?"

For a moment Lois stared over Diane's head as though concentrating on something that might indicate how to word her next statement. "I might as well tell you right away that Gordon's adamant about her not living with us."

Diane said nothing. Having just voiced objections of her own, how could she possibly criticize Gordon? Yet it would obviously be easier for them than for her to take Ella. For one thing, their house was large enough so that Ella could have her own quarters and they wouldn't all be on top of each other. For another, as a full-time homemaker and faculty wife Lois didn't exactly lead an arduous life, especially now that Amy was in boarding school and Ned— well, Ned wasn't at home. It was true that Lois kept busy with a certain amount of volunteer work, sat on various boards and committees. Lately, too, she had taken up—watercolor? Weaving? Something like that. But her time was her own, to apportion as she chose. Still, if Gordon was definitely set against it—but was that actually the case, or was Gordon only an excuse?

"As you know," Lois said, "there isn't money to waste, but Ella won't be a financial burden."

True. As co-executors Lois and Diane were to divide the contents of the house and Fay's personal effects between them, after allocating to Ella whatever she wanted or might need. Fay's jewelry, of intrinsic value only, would go to Amy. Everything else would go to Ella, to be used for her benefit—proceeds from the sale of the house, insurance, some stock, funds in the bank, though not a great deal.

But Lois knew very well, of course, that her—Diane's— reluctance had nothing to do with money.

"Put it this way," Diane said. "If Gordon changed his mind, would you be willing to take her?"

"That's a very large if." Lois came and sat down. "There is another possibility, though. One that might be better, in fact. For Ella and all of us."

Diane hesitated. "Not an institution. Ella's not—"

"Of course not! Give me some credit, I'm not entirely without—"

"I'm sorry," Diane said hastily. "That was silly of me. What do you have in mind?"

"I've talked to someone at the Reese Developmental Center. There are group residences for people like Ella, people who can function in a limited way but can't live alone. To qualify, Ella would have to be in one of the center's programs, working or going to school."

"But then how—"

The center found jobs for people like Ella, Lois explained. With the training Ella had had from Fay, she could probably work in food service, in a cafeteria perhaps, helping with the cooking, or in a bakery.

It wasn't a bad idea, Diane thought, as Lois went on talking. Under Fay's direction, Ella had become quite proficient; under supervision, she could probably manage the simple tasks that would be required of her.

"Well? What do you think? She'd have to go to the center for an interview."

"Sounds promising. If she's willing to try. You know how she is about strangers."

Lois threw up her hands. " 'Slightly retarded' doesn't mean 'helpless.' It's too bad Mother babied her so. I'm convinced she could have done a lot more than Mother expected of her."

"That's not fair, Lois. Mother did a good thing when she trained Ella to help her. I'm sure it's because of Ella that she started the catering business instead of going back to teaching."

"On the other hand, letting Ella stay home in a kind of cocoon may not have been the best thing for her. Look, you can always do more with Ella than I can. If I make an appointment at the center, will you persuade her to go there with us?"

"I'll try."

Lois's mouth tightened. "You should make it clear she really doesn't have a choice."

Diane thought privately that a better approach was to present the job possibility as a pleasant prospect, as indeed it might be. Ella took pride in her culinary skill.

Lois was right: this was worth pursuing. It would be good for Ella to develop a life of her own. Diane had a sudden picture of Ella going off to work each morning, scurrying along with that duck-footed walk.

"All right, Lo, I'll talk to her. Meanwhile—" She broke off as the room was suddenly lit greenish white. A crash of thunder sounded, then rain began thrumming at the windows, quietly at first, then rapidly louder.

"Is everything closed upstairs?" Lois asked.

"Yes. Listen."

The rocking had stopped. Footsteps sounded overhead as Ella rushed to the window to watch the storm. She was always excited by this kind of weather; she would stand at the window as long as it lasted, gazing out as though hypnotized.

Suddenly through the pelting of the rain came another sound.

"Was that the doorbell?"

"Yes," Lois said. "That's probably—"

Diane nodded, stood up, and hurried through the rooms that were shadowed now with the gloom of the storm.

CHAPTER 2 . . .

Diane opened the door and switched on the porch light. The man standing there stepped forward, and she saw rain trickling down his face like tears.

"You're getting drenched! Come in."

For an instant he hesitated. Then he stepped inside.

She closed the door. "My sister's the one who knows about the piano. She's the one you should talk to."

Just then Lois appeared and gave him a politely encouraging smile. "This way."

He followed them into the living room, where Lois switched on the floor lamp that stood by the piano. "You might want to have it voiced, but the board's intact, and these are the original ivories. Try it."

Seeming tentative, he put a hand on the keys and pressed a chord till the notes sounded softly in the room's stillness. For a moment he stood in a listening attitude, head turned sideways. Then he straightened up without playing further and put his hands in his pockets. "I'm afraid there's—a misunderstanding." His tone was slightly apologetic. "I'm not here about the piano."

"Not—?"

His next words amazed them. "So you're Lois. And—are you Diane?"

Diane glanced at her sister. *Someone we should know?*

Lois looked baffled. "Have we met?"

"Well—you see—"

It's some kind of sales gimmick, Diane thought. He's gotten our names off a list, and he's selling siding or storm windows. Or perhaps casing the place for a future burglary?

"I'm Charlie Hazzard."

The words seemed to hang in the air without shape or meaning. The rain beating at the windows emphasized the silence.

Lois, her voice pitched at an incredulous squeak, said, *"What?"*

It's all right, you misheard him, so did I, Diane wanted to say.

"Charlie Hazzard," he repeated politely, as though supplying the words because someone had said, I didn't quite catch—?

Lois seemed transfixed.

Diane finally found her voice. "You said"—she cleared her throat—"did you say—"

"Yes."

She stared.

Was it some sort of trick? A con game? But why would anyone lie about this? What would be gained? On the other hand, there were some strange types around. "Can you show us—some kind of identification?"

He smiled faintly. "Driver's license? Social Security card?"

"Well—yes."

He produced his wallet.

There it was: Charles B. Hazzard. What did the B. stand for? she wondered.

"Let me see that!" Lois said.

She saw. Then, like a dam breaking, words burst from her.

"And you have the—the unmitigated gall, the colossal nerve, to walk in just like that, uninvited!"

"I beg your pardon," he said quietly. "I was invited."

"You know perfectly well what I mean! You wouldn't have been allowed to set foot in this house if we'd known who you were!"

"Is that true?" He looked inquiringly from one to the other.

Diane, her mind in a whirl, tried to consider. For Lois, the answer was obvious. For herself—who knew? Would she have let him in? Would curiosity, if nothing else, have betrayed her into letting this happen?

"Why did you come?"

"Oh, that's easy!" Lois's voice was heavy with contempt. "He heard about Mother. He thought a visit might be worth his while. Perhaps there was something here for him. Perhaps he could put in a claim of some kind."

"I knew Fay had died, yes," he said mildly. "But as for claiming—"

"You're here because you missed us, then?" Lois's lip curled.

He said, slowly, "I wanted to see you. To see . . . how you were getting on."

"Were you very worried about us, then, after—let's see—thirty-three years?"

"Worried? No, it wasn't that." He had decided, Diane saw, to treat Lois's words as though she meant them literally. "It was simply—I wanted to look you up. Make your acquaintance."

"Couldn't you find a better story than that?" Lois asked.

"It happens to be true. I'm sorry you don't believe me." He shifted his weight from one foot to the other. "Could we sit down? It's difficult to talk when—"

"I hardly think—"

"Yes, let's sit down," Diane said. Despite everything, she was curious to hear what he had to say, fiction though it might be.

Charles moved toward the sofa and began to sit, but then he

25

straightened up again. "Sorry, I'm damp. I won't do the upholstery much good." Water dripped from the hem of his raincoat.

"Give me that." Diane took the raincoat out to the hall and hung it on the coatrack. Returning, she sat down in the armchair and studied him openly. Not big to start with, he seemed even smaller now, diminished by the size of the sofa. Ordinary, innocuous, he would never be noticed in a crowd, or out of it. She would have expected him to look more—special somehow, though she couldn't have said how. The other surprising aspect was his manner: whatever his real reason might be for this visit, he seemed amazingly self-assured, considering the circumstances. Tired, yes, but composed. Yet how could he possibly be composed? How, in fact, could he *be*?

He reached in his pocket and took out a pack of cigarettes. "Do you mind—?"

"I certainly do," Lois said. "In any case, don't get too comfortable, this will be a short session. Let's be frank." She folded her arms. "Your motives are perfectly clear. To me, anyway. To put it bluntly"—her tone became falsely conversational—"you're not getting any younger. And you're . . . down on your luck, perhaps? You thought there might be something here to latch on to. Perhaps one of us could be persuaded to do something for you. Take you in. Give you a home. That's it, isn't it?"

Diane suddenly felt acutely uncomfortable. Lois might be right. But if she were, and if he were forced to admit it, the admission would be no more pleasant for them—for her, Diane, anyway—than for him. Any denial would be equally embarrassing.

He seemed to be considering Lois's words.

"No. Not exactly," he said, finally.

His self-possession, the absence of any trace of guilt or nervousness, seemed to anger Lois further.

"*Approximately*, then. I might not have gotten all the details right. I don't know which of us you thought might welcome you, fling her arms around you crying, 'Father! Home at last!' Or perhaps you had visions of some kind of rotation plan, spending part of the year with each of us?"

His glance rested on her thoughtfully. "If that were true, what would my chances be of success?"

"About what you'd expect."

His glance went to Diane. "That goes for you, too?"

After a moment she nodded.

"Of course, there's my third hope, isn't there?"

For the first time Lois smiled. "I wouldn't give much for your chances there."

"I see." He leaned his head back against the sofa and closed his eyes.

The light from the lamp caught traces of moisture on his forehead. Perhaps, after all, he wasn't quite so self-possessed as he appeared, Diane thought.

His eyes opened. He sat up straight. "You wouldn't care to offer me a little refreshment, would you? Without prejudice, of course, as the lawyers say."

"My, you're a cool customer!" Lois said. "Sorry, we weren't expecting the return of the prodigal father, or we'd have laid in a stock."

But Diane suddenly realized that a drink was exactly what she herself could do with. She stood up. "We have some vodka, that's all—"

"For heaven's sake, don't apologize to him!"

"What I'd really like is coffee," he said. "If that's possible?"

Cool customer was right, Diane thought. Almost, she could admire him. "Do you want something, Lois?"

"No, thanks. Not in this company."

Diane went to the kitchen and started making coffee. The rain had begun to abate, she noticed. But now, as though warning that the storm was still to be reckoned with, a muttering rumble sounded, and the downpour resumed with fresh vigor. Waiting for the coffee, Diane poured herself a drink. Then she went into the dining room and looked out the window. Yes, there stood a car, small, foreign, neither old nor new nor in any way special, just a means of transportation. Anonymous, like him. Was it his? Was it rented? From here she couldn't see the license plate. Where had he come from?

Carrying the coffee into the living room, she heard Lois putting just that question. "Did you come very far, in your—er— anxiety about our welfare?"

"From the Coast." He took the coffee with murmured thanks. California. Had he been there all this time? Curiosity over- rode feelings of anger. The situation was, more than anything, strangely intriguing. For some reason, she felt as though this were happening to someone else; she felt like a bystander, listening, observing, while someone else was telling the story. And then what happened? she wanted to ask. And why did—? And what prompted—? The desire to know, to fill in the blanks that had existed all these years, was far stronger than the need to reproach.

But by the same token, she felt no warmth for him either, filial or otherwise, no personal feeling at all for this stranger blown in with the storm. Father. He had fathered her, yes, in the sense that he and Fay together had made her, and Lois, and Ella. He had lived in this house all those years ago, had probably watched as Lois, and then she, Diane, had crept, walked, talked, in this very room. But it still seemed impossible to believe. Anyway, that history signified nothing: they—she—had never known him, did not know him now, this small, tired-looking, elderly man who sat here drinking coffee. Lois was right, he was by now a total stranger. Even less than a stranger, for they would have had no grievance against a stranger. If that now seemed hard, he had only himself to thank. He had made his choice a long time ago. They owed him nothing. The shoe was on the other foot. And clearly Lois was going to make sure it stayed there.

"Thank you. That was very good, Diane."

As he set down his cup, she saw that his hand trembled slightly. Just a physical tremor, a palsy of age? Or was he, after all, more nervous than he appeared? Whichever, he suddenly seemed vulnerable, and therefore real. At the same time, she was oddly disconcerted at hearing him use her name so easily. He was obviously trying to put this on a more personal footing; this was his not so subtle way of reminding her that they were, like it or not, related.

She sat bolt upright. "What is it you want, exactly?"

He moved his hand, as if groping for the right words. "I had some free time. I thought I'd look you up."

"For 'free time,' read 'at loose ends,' " Lois said. "For 'look you up,' read 'investigate the possibilities.' "

"You really think so?"

Lois stared back at him. "It's true, isn't it?"

"Well—yes. In a way. But—" He paused.

"But what?" Diane prompted. "Would you be more explicit?"

"Pound of flesh?" He gave her a quick, upward glance. "All right. Here I am, getting on in years—"

"And—alone?" Lois's voice was mocking.

"Yes, alone, though I—"

The telephone rang.

"I'll get it," Lois said. "I've heard enough of this."

Diane waited until she was gone. "How did you know about Mother?"

"I saw the obituary. What did she die of?"

There could be no harm in saying, surely. "A stroke. She was paralyzed for a while first."

"That's dreadful. I'm sorry." He paused. "I can't picture it, she was always so strong. In every way."

Her own thought exactly—though he, Diane suddenly realized, was referring to a much younger woman.

"Do you live here? In the house?"

"No. But when Mother fell ill, I—" She stopped. Why was he

asking all these questions? Why, for that matter, was she answering? Why was she talking to him at all? She could imagine what Fay would have felt if she'd known he was here, if she had heard Diane conversing with him like this. She must stop this at once. As soon as Lois came back, they would send him away.

The rain was still coming down. She heard it at the windows and in the sounds made by passing vehicles, their tires slapping against the wet pavement. She thought again of the car out there, visualized him getting in that car moments from now and driving off. Where? Not directly back to California, necessarily. Where, then, tonight? Did he have a friend in town, after all this time? Someone who had sent him the obituary? Here, or in California or somewhere else, was someone waiting for him? A woman? Wife? Or were they to believe what he'd said about being alone? Alone, getting on in years . . . The stuff of cheap melodrama, violins sobbing. Lois was right.

Yet when he spoke again, she again found herself replying.

"Are you married, Diane?"

"No."

"Lois is married, I gather."

He must have noticed her ring. "Anything you want to know about Lois, you must ask her directly."

He raised a hand to his ear and pulled the lobe absently.

From somewhere deep in a past that she had forgotten she had even forgotten, there came a dim recollection of just such a gesture—the hand going up, finger and thumb tugging gently. . . .

Nonsense. She couldn't possibly be recalling such a thing. She'd been less than two years old. But suddenly a bridge of sorts seemed forged with the past. A tenuous link.

His next words seemed to strengthen it.

"Does the leg still fall off that stool when you move it? I never could get it to stay."

She gazed at the footstool with the maroon plush seat that had stood by the fireplace for as long as she could remember. So it was true: this elderly man, with the measured voice, faded eyes, shirt collar that stood away from his neck, had once lived here. Had been married to Fay. With Fay had conceived Lois and Ella and . . .

Overwhelmed, she was unable to speak.

Had he guessed what she was feeling? For as though pressing home an advantage, he said quickly, "Would you put me up for the next few days?"

"Put you up? *Here?*"

"Just till I make some plans, decide—"

"What's wrong with a motel?"

"Four bedrooms here, if I remember correctly. Can't you spare me one for a night or two?"

She felt her face go warm with annoyance and embarrassment. "That's not the point, as—"

"Just for tonight?"

Lois returned. "That was Mario. I said you'd call back."

Charles kept his gaze on Diane. "Well?"

She shook her head. And stood.

He waited a moment, but no one spoke. Moving slowly, he got to his feet. "I'll be on my way then."

Silence.

He turned and walked out to the hall. Diane and Lois followed. He put on his raincoat; it was still wet and difficult to handle. He fumbled with it.

"Here—let me—" Diane moved forward to help. His hand brushed hers as it came through the sleeve.

He moved to the door, then halted. "Is this all?"

"Listen." Lois's voice rang with certainty. "Many years ago you decided our need for you wasn't nearly so important as your need to leave. So you went. Our needs, our lives meant nothing to you. You made no attempt to support us or stay in touch—"

"How do you know?"

Lois turned white. "I know this much—we managed to

survive without you, thanks to Mother. And now we can take care of ourselves. You're not needed anymore. Or wanted."

"You don't believe in mincing words."

"Oh, come on," Diane said. "Fair's fair, after all. Don't cast yourself as the injured party. You can hardly drop in after all this time and expect to be welcomed."

"The fact that I'm your father means nothing?"

"It meant nothing to *you*," Lois said, "all those years ago."

"I see." A moment passed. "Well, I won't trouble you further. You won't hear from me again."

He opened the door. Beyond, the rain descended in solid sheets. Spray fountained from beneath the wheels of a passing car.

Looking at the torrent, Diane was appalled. She heard herself say weakly, "Do you have far to go?"

He did something that affected her as no words could have done: he shrugged. Without a backward glance, he stepped outside. His raincoat swung open, unheeded.

"Oh, wait—let—an umbrella—"

But he went on down the steps, through the rain, not looking back. Perhaps he hadn't heard?

They watched him get in the car and settle behind the wheel. They heard the engine cough as he turned on the ignition. It failed to catch. He tried it again and again. Now the engine wouldn't even turn over.

He got out of the car and came back up the steps, his sparse hair plastered wetly to his scalp.

"I'm afraid the battery's dead. May I use your phone to call a service station?"

Lois was silent.

Diane said, "Yes, there's a place half a mile from here. The phone's in the kitchen."

She showed him the telephone, gave him the number, then rejoined Lois in the hall. From there they listened to him explain, heard him give the address and hang up.

He came out to the hall. "They're sending someone. I'll wait in the car."

"Fine," Lois said.

"Lois, there's no need—" Diane drew a deep breath. "Look, you can stay here tonight. But you'll have to leave without fail tomorrow."

Lois's jaw dropped. "Are you out of your mind?"

"This is up to me, Lois. We're each old enough to make our own decisions."

From above came the sound of a door opening. Seconds later Ella's tall, angular figure came into view, clumping noisily down the stairs.

CHAPTER 3 • • •

Lois was hardly aware of traffic as she drove, or of signals winking ruby, amber, and emerald through the waterlogged landscape. Like sparks struck from an anvil, her thoughts flew off in all directions. Too late, she realized she had passed her exit. By the time she reached home she had been on the road for nearly an hour instead of the twenty-five minutes it normally took from Fay's.

As she pulled up in the circular driveway, she felt so drained that she couldn't summon the energy to get out of the car. It was stress, of course, the cumulative effects of the past several months, capped by today's bizarre development. "Bizarre" was right. The mere thought of it refueled her anger. At him, and even more at Diane. Where was Diane's sense of fitness, of loyalty? Was she naive, or simply uncaring, to let that man spend even one night in Fay's house?

Lost in thought, she remained in the car until the rain lessened. Gradually the scene before her came back into focus: this house, her lovely house . . .

They had bought this place just before Amy was born. It was set between tall locust trees, with a willow-bordered brook

meandering across the property. From the moment she first laid eyes
on it, she had known it was the kind of home she wanted, the kind
of house in which they'd be happy. The previous place had been all
right, but with Amy coming along they needed more room, and
Gordon wanted enough acreage so they could put in a pool and a
tennis court. The house itself was conventional—large white colo-
nial, black shutters, red door—but attractive nonetheless. Nonetheless? The point was—and this was something her mother had
never understood—she was happy with convention, a conventional
life; she welcomed the structure convention imposed, the shape it
gave to daily existence. If that ruled out a certain excitement, made
for routine and a narrower range, so be it. Where would she wander,
anyway, given no restrictions or restraints?

If she had ever said that in front of Fay and Diane, she knew
exactly how those two would have glanced at each other. Her
mother had had little concern for convention. And Diane always
deliberately flouted it, so far as Lois could see. Those men she got
involved with—the yoga teacher, the radical Venezuelan poet, the
French journalist. Heaven forbid she should ever take up with any
of the captains of industry she met in her work. And that neighborhood she lived in, though she earned a perfectly adequate
income . . . How Diane lived was entirely her own business, of
course, but it was just as well she and Diane lived in different
cities.

•   •   •

Indoors, Lois found a note from Dora Mae on the kitchen counter.
"Mrs. Norris called, will call again tomorrow. Mr. Burke won't be
home till 7:30."

She looked through the mail. Two more condolence notes, a
letter from Gordon's aunt in Hilton Head, and a letter from Amy.
Nothing from Ned.

She went upstairs, taking Amy's letter with her. She would
read it after she'd gotten out of her clothes and taken a shower.

Amy didn't write often; like most people nowadays and certainly most teenagers, she preferred to pick up the telephone and call. So a letter from Amy was always a special treat, something to be saved the way you'd save the last dollop of béarnaise on a rare filet, the last chocolate chip in a cookie.

You couldn't describe any of those occasional communications from Ned as a treat, those one or two lines scribbled on a postcard, or on a dog-eared page torn out of a pad, or on the back of one of those sub shop flyers you find tucked under your windshield. "Rain, rain, go away, I'm A-okay." Or: "Coming to you live from the bottom of the barrel!" Or: "Going along, getting along, love to Amy-Mamy." A mixed message, according to Dr. Lyman. On the one hand, Help me. On the other, Leave me alone. Nevertheless, she was always thankful to get them, grateful for the fact that he was at least staying in touch.

She had been partially distracted from her worry over Ned while Fay was ill, but since her mother's death, all her attention had reverted to this problem. It did no good, of course. She realized that. In addition, she needed all her resources now for other matters, such as getting Ella settled and the house disposed of. And she owed it to Gordon and Amy to carry on with a normal day-to-day routine, no matter how she might be feeling. She wanted to keep up with her pots, too.

When Dr. Lyman had first said, Take a course, find a hobby, treat yourself to something you'll enjoy, she had thought, Does he really think stenciling or Italian for Beginners will make me feel better? But Dr. Lyman pressed, as did Gordon, so finally she signed up for a ceramics course. As her skill increased, her interest grew until she used the course not for therapy but for pleasure in the thing itself. It was like magic every time, watching the wheel spin, the amorphous lump at the center running up fast, to become whatever she chose it to be. Then Marge Norris had taken her in as a partner at The Potter's Shed. This gave her not only an ideal place to work but a place where people came to see what she made, and even to buy from time to time. The fact that there were people who liked her work enough to pay for it brought great satisfaction.

Had Fay derived similar feelings from successfully selling what she made? Lois wished she had understood that earlier. As a teenager she had always been faintly ashamed of her mother's business. She had helped, of course, when she was still at home, but she had never told anyone. If she couldn't go out because Fay needed help with the catering, she always told her friends she had to help with the housework or errands. The very word *catering* seemed to her to have a connotation of *menial*. Even when they cooked for the most elegant occasions, she still felt embarrassed to think her mother did this for a living. Whenever she watched Fay working, wearing her butcher apron, sleeves rolled up, face hard with concentration, she kept wishing Fay had remained a piano teacher.

As she grew older, that feeling persisted. She had hemmed and hawed about her mother's business when she first met Gordon and was relieved to find that he seemed impressed rather than disdainful. "You mean, your mother's done well enough to support you all and send you to college?"

He was right, of course; it was an achievement. She kept wishing now that she had talked to Fay about it. It might have helped bring them closer. It might have offset the differences they'd had, about many things, including Lois's marriage. After she and Gordon were actually married, Fay had never said another word against it—to her, anyway—but Lois had always known how she felt. It had something to do with what had happened to Fay's own marriage, she supposed. And bringing up three children alone couldn't have been exactly fun, either—she couldn't think why else her mother would have turned on her so angrily when Lois told her she was pregnant. "Already!" As though they'd been careless. When Lois told her they had planned this pregnancy, Fay said no more, but her face got that mottled look that was easy to interpret. Lois felt terribly hurt. She told Fay she had somehow had the crazy idea that parents were supposed to be happy to become grandparents; then she'd flung out of Fay's house and hadn't called her for weeks. Yet she had to admit that from the day Ned was born, Fay took him to her heart—and Amy, too, in due course—as warmly as any traditional grandmother would.

. . .

Traditional wasn't a term you could generally apply to her mother. Lois had spent her adolescence privately bemoaning that fact. In those days, of course, she had been critical of almost everything about Fay. To start with, she couldn't stand the way Fay raised her voice whenever something bothered her—even in public, never caring who might hear. She couldn't bear the way Fay laughed, that loud, explosive sound that went on too long. She squirmed with embarrassment at the way Fay always fell into talk with strangers—anyone, the woman who sold stamps at the post office, people at the farmers' market, the man who came to repair the oven. Did she always have to lounge in any chair she sat in, an arm thrown carelessly over the back, taking up more space than necessary? Why couldn't she sit tidily, legs neatly crossed, like other girls' mothers? Her legs were pretty, and she looked quite different on the rare occasions she wore high heels and nylons. Why couldn't she wear dresses more often, instead of those awful baggy slacks and shapeless, peasanty-looking tops?

Lois longed for her mother to comport herself with greater dignity and reserve. When that didn't happen, Lois herself made a point of behaving in a way she felt was low-key, restrained, dignified, so as to seem as unlike Fay as possible. She would give no one any reason to say she resembled this woman who happened to be her mother.

. . .

A week after Fay's stroke, they had all been with her in the hospital when a single tear brimmed from her functioning eye and rolled down her cheek. As Ella leaned forward and wiped it away, Lois realized suddenly that this was the only time she had ever seen her mother cry. She had seen her angry, often, but she had never seen her weep. There must have been times when she'd wept, surely? When her husband left? When Ella was born? But somehow, Lois couldn't picture her sobbing, helpless and hopeless. Fay had a will of iron, and she had used that iron against her eldest daughter far more often than she'd shown her love. But even so, there was tenderness in Fay, too. For Ella always. And for Ned and Amy. And, yes, for Lois, too, before she'd married, though Lois had rarely responded back then, caught up as she was in the toils and moils of mother-daughter antagonism. But after Lois married, Fay seemed to write her off; whatever affection she had had for Lois, she seemed to transfer after that to Diane.

· · ·

Lois had told Fay the truth when she said she had planned to become pregnant early on. Still, she hadn't enjoyed her first pregnancy. She had felt fine physically, but secretly she worried for the whole term. No matter what the doctor said, how could she help it, with a sister like Ella? She had felt enormous relief, as well as joy, when Ned was born healthy and normal in all respects. The first time Ned was placed in her arms, she inspected him thoroughly, every inch of his tiny body, arms and legs, fingers and toes, eyes, ears, shape of his head, everything. As the weeks and months passed, she watched him closely, checking off each stage of his mental and physical development . . . his first responses to outside stimuli, first sounds, first words, first movements, the first time he managed to turn over, crawl, pull himself up, take a step—all on schedule, thank God, and sometimes sooner. Only then had she fully understood what it must have been like for Fay to bear a child like Ella and to carry that burden alone, her husband having taken off months before. Which certainly had something to do with the fact that Ella was born prematurely, brain-damaged. One of a number of things for which she, Lois, would never forgive the man who called himself her father.

His face today, as Ella came down the stairs and he realized . . .

Of course, there's my third hope, kept running through her head. For a moment she had felt almost sorry for him.

Halfway down, Ella had halted, staring. "Who's that?" she asked, in her queer, hoarse voice.

Lois had felt a certain grim satisfaction as she waited for what was bound to happen.

Ella had always been leery of strangers, especially males. It was months before she had ever done more than stare suspiciously at Gordon. Finally one day she had walked over to him, raised her foot, and stamped down hard on his cordovan loafers. Gordon yelped with pain and collapsed into the nearest chair. No bones were broken, but from then on he gave up trying to make friends with her. Perversely, the minute he stopped trying, Ella decided he was all right, and started, in her own fashion, almost making up to him. But it was too late, so far as Gordon was concerned; afterward he always edged away whenever she went near him.

She had given Mario an even harder time. She'd decided that Mario was an enemy, *the* enemy, when she first laid eyes on him, several years back. Which was the first time Lois had met him, too. She had stopped by to see Fay that afternoon while Amy was at her riding lesson. Fay and Ella had just finished a large party order, which was due to be picked up at six. At five-thirty Fay, Lois, and Ella were all in the kitchen, Fay with a glass of the dry vermouth she liked, Lois with tea, and Ella with an orange soda, when Mario came by.

"Lois, this is Mario Rossi," Fay said. "Mario, this is my daughter Lois Burke. And this is Ella."

Lois thought at first that he had come to pick up the order. Rossi. It sounded familiar. A restaurant, perhaps? Fay supplied a number of restaurants.

"Hi, there. Pleased to meet you, Lois." He shook her hand.

"Hello, Ella, how's tricks?" He had a deep, fruity voice—not gay, literally fruity, juicy as a pineapple. When he smiled, Lois saw the gleam of a gold cap. There was considerable gold about him: he wore a gold ring set with onyx; his shirt, which was open several buttons' worth, revealed gold chains decorating his curly gray chest hair.

"How about a drink?" Fay asked him.

"That would hit the spot." He went into the pantry and helped himself.

Only then did Lois understand that, whoever, whatever, he hadn't come for the order. And this might be the first time he'd met Ella, but he had obviously been here before—he knew exactly where everything was.

"Can I get anyone a refill?" he called.

"We're taken care of," Fay called back.

Lois noticed then that her mother had taken off her apron. While Mario was still in the pantry, Fay quickly pulled the pins from her hair and shook it loose around her face.

Mario came back with a drink and sat down, sprawling at ease, legs wide apart, in that graceless fashion some men have, making himself very much at home. Fay looked at him. He smiled back. Suddenly, though he and Fay were nowhere near each other, Lois felt acutely uncomfortable. There was something in her mother's face that shouldn't have been revealed in front of any third party. Not that she disapproved of Fay's having a relationship, God knows. She had always hoped Fay would eventually settle down with someone suitable. But—*this* man? Quite apart from every-thing else, he seemed to be in his late forties, at least ten years Fay's junior.

"You've been busy, Fay." He indicated the lineup of filled boxes on the counter.

"Yes. And you?"

"A madhouse. You know how Fridays are. Good thing I took on that new guy."

"What do you do, Mr. Rossi?" Lois asked.

The gold tooth flashed. "Mario, please." He handed her a card.

She looked at it. Now she knew why the name was familiar: she had friends who went to him to have their hair done.

"I just picked up a bunch of new records, Fay. How about coming over this evening?"

"Tonight?" Fay looked doubtfully in Ella's direction. "I don't know whether Alice can come."

Alice was a widow who earned a little money doing what she called "people-sitting." Apart from Lois and Diane, she was the only person Ella would occasionally agree to be left with.

"Give her a call. We'll—"

Before he could say another word, Ella rushed over to him and, shrieking something unintelligible, grabbed the gold chains and began to tug.

"Hey, hey!" Mario cried, his face reddening as his head was jerked forward. He tried to fend Ella off, but she hung on doggedly. The two of them rocked back and forth like partners engaged in a ritualistic dance.

"Ella, stop!" Fay shouted. "Stop that at once! Ella!"

Lois was so astonished she could only gape.

Fay tried to pull Ella away, but Ella continued tugging with one hand while she used the other to pound Mario about the head.

He managed to break free, finally. Struggling to keep her away without hurting her, he sat her down forcibly in one of the chairs. She immediately burst into loud, racking sobs—though no tears came from her eyes, Lois noticed.

"Ella, what's the matter with you? Tell Mario you're sorry!" For once, Fay seemed angry with her.

"It's all right, Fay, there's no harm done." He sounded out of breath. He passed his hands over his disheveled hair, then did up all the buttons of his shirt, concealing the chains.

Ella jumped to her feet and ran from the kitchen. They heard her rush upstairs. Then the door of her room slammed with such force that a mixing bowl bounced off its hook on the wall.

● ● ●

Now, as Ella continued down the stairs, gazing fixedly at Charles, Lois held her breath.

"Ella, this is"—Diane hesitated—"this is Charles. Charlie. This is Ella," she said to him.

Charles and Ella inspected each other.

Suddenly Ella loped toward him. Lois was sure she was about to attack him, but instead she moved close and, stooping slightly—she was considerably taller—placed an arm around his shoulders.

Lois was flabbergasted. So, clearly, was Diane.

After a second Charles, looking somewhat tentative, reached up and patted Ella's hand. "You and I are going to be friends, Ella."

She gave one of her rasping giggles. Then she put up her other hand and stroked his face.

The scene was ludicrous and all at once, for some reason, unbearably sad. Lois couldn't stand to go on watching.

"All right, this is *your* doing, you handle it!" she told Diane. "I'll have nothing more to do with it."

And she left.

● ● ●

Alone in the restful silence of her house, she took a lengthy shower. It helped. By the time she was done, she was feeling calmer. She put on a robe and sat down to read Amy's letter.

This was the first word from Amy since she'd gone back to school after the funeral. Fay had been cremated, her ashes scattered on the river where it narrowed and flowed through a wooded section of Larimer Park. The silently moving waters had at once absorbed all that was left of the temporal Fay, leaving only memories, some of which would be carried away by the flow of time just as her ashes were carried off by the water, while some would stay forever in the consciousness of those who had known her. Lois had tried to say that to a weeping Amy afterward, to console her. But she hadn't done it well. She'd been left with the feeling that she'd somehow been inadequate. That feeling seemed confirmed as she read Amy's rounded script.

> . . . After I got back, I just kept crying at first. But I'm glad I was there. The thought of burning up was really scarey, but afterward I thought that's better than lying in the ground with—you know, the worms crawl in, the worms crawl out. This way, it's over quickly and it's good for the environment. It was sad when the ashes were scattered, but it was beautiful, too, out there in the open, with the trees reflected in the water.
>
> I have a new friend here, her name's Rachna, she's from India. She has one of those red dots on her forehead. Her father works for the United Nations. She told me her sister died last year, and she couldn't stop crying when it first happened. But you're supposed to cry, crying helps you heal, she said. That's really true, because I'm beginning to feel better. . . .

Unlike Lois, Rachna seemed to have found the right words. Lois sighed and put the letter on Gordon's bureau. The best thing about a letter as opposed to a phone call was that it was tangible, to have and to keep, to read over again whenever you wished.

How she missed Amy. Initially she had opposed Amy's going away to school this year, but Amy had pleaded to go, and Gordon had ultimately supported Amy in this, though he, too, missed her. Of course, these days Gordon would support Amy in almost anything. Lois understood, because she, too, had come to an even greater appreciation of this daughter who was living proof that parenthood could bring pleasure as well as pain.

Amy. Ned. How could they be so different? Amy, four years younger, was sunny and outgoing. In adversity she often dissolved in tears, but the storm was brief, and when it was over, it was done, finished. Ned, on the other hand, brooded forever; he never seemed able to let go of anything. Back in fifth grade, when his best friend, Zack, had moved away, you'd have thought the world had ended. It was true Ned and Zack had been friends since kindergarden; they spent as much time in each other's houses as they did in their own. Ned followed Zack in everything, catching frogs, joining Cub Scouts, favoring the same books, the same television programs. It was only natural that he'd feel bereft at first. But he'd moped around for months, stayed in his room, wouldn't bother with other friends.

"Shouldn't he be getting over it by now?" Gordon had asked. "Kids that age usually get over that sort of thing pretty fast."

"You know how Ned takes everything to heart," Lois had said. Gordon clearly didn't understand that the minor tragedies of life could seem major at that age. In any case, Ned didn't get over anything pretty fast.

It was the same years later, when Ned injured his knee and couldn't play soccer anymore.

"The way he's acting, you'd think a brilliant career had been terminated," Gordon said. "He wasn't even very good at soccer, in my opinion."

"He's disappointed, Gordon."

"Yes, but life's full of disappointments. He has to learn to cut his losses and go on to something else."

Different though they were, Ned and Amy had always been friends and allies. It went both ways, not just Ned's looking out for his sister but Amy's standing up for Ned. When Ned, at thirteen, broke a neighbor's window while fooling around with a BB gun, Gordon came down on him hard, but Amy gallantly defended him. "It was just an accident, Dad. You can't blame someone for an accident." Ned had to apologize to the neighbors, of course, and pay for the window. Lois knew that Amy had offered Ned the six dollars she'd saved up to buy a rabbit.

The following year, when Ned, with some others, was suspended after being caught smoking marijuana on school premises, Gordon was icily furious. Lois was angry, too. But Gordon's anger took the form not only of curfews and privileges denied but of ostracizing Ned. This seemed to her inhuman. It would have been better to rage at Ned than subject him to a frigid silence that reduced him to a nonperson.

But by the time Ned was in his last year of high school, he seemed to have settled down nicely. He had taken up classical guitar, which naturally pleased Fay. And he was on the swim team. He was even doing fairly well academically, though he'd never been a scholar.

Lois gave much of the credit for this change to Karen. Ned and Karen had been going out together since they were barely sixteen. Karen was not especially pretty, but she was gentle and sweet and rather shy, in an old-fashioned way. She was an excellent student and seemed a positive influence on Ned in this respect as well as others. Ned plainly adored her. When he was with her, he seemed happier, more assured, more at ease with himself. When the time came for college, he scrapped an earlier plan to apply to Northwestern, where Gordon had once taught, and applied instead to the small liberal arts school where Karen planned to go. Gordon took a dim view of choosing a college on this basis, and Lois voiced some doubts, too, but Ned wouldn't be swayed.

The summer before he left, Amy mourned the prospect of her brother's departure. He kept reminding her that he wouldn't be far away. "Just a hundred and twenty miles, Amy-Mamy. You'll come to visit. I'll be coming home a lot, too, with Karen."

And for a while things had gone as promised.

• • •

Six-thirty.

Lois went downstairs to start dinner: soup, lamb chops, salad. There was a little pâté left over from the weekend, when they'd had people in from the department; she put it out for Gordon to have with a drink. After he'd had a chance to catch his breath, she would tell him what had happened today.

What was happening over there right now? Were they sitting talking, he and Diane? Was Ella with them, listening? What room would Diane put him in tonight? Not Fay's—surely she wouldn't be that insensitive. In any case, Ella wouldn't stand for it; she wouldn't yield that room to anyone. On the other hand, the way Ella had cozied up to him, who could say what she would allow? Unbelievable, the way she'd behaved. She couldn't possibly have known who he was. He was simply a stranger to whom, inexplicably, she had taken a liking. A stranger, yes, to all of them. It took more than biology for people to be more than strangers to each other.

. . .

When Gordon came home, she knew, before he'd said a word, that his meeting hadn't gone well. He had a habit of taking off his glasses and rubbing his eyes whenever something bothered him— an unconscious gesture that always left his eyes looking pink. Just now they were almost painfully reddened.

She watched him as he poured a drink. Time had not been unkind to him; at fifty-nine, he had no jowls, dewlaps, or extra chins, and she wished her stomach were as flat as his. But over the past year his hair had turned white, and his face was full of hollows. Whenever she saw him naked, the sight of his flattened buttocks, his shanks thinned almost to an old man's fragility moved her to mixed feelings of compassion and regret. What did he feel when he saw *her* naked? She'd noticed he seemed to avoid that sight. And more than the sight—they hadn't made love for several months. Her fault as much as his, she supposed. You can't make love when resentment's growing inside you like a tumor. Her tumor had been growing for a long time now, over the business of Ned. Over the fact that Gordon had simply withdrawn, left her alone with the problem.

"That's enough," he'd said firmly. "There's no point going on talking about it, day after day."

"No *point?*"

"You heard what Dr. Lyman said—we have to get back on an even keel, we can't stop functioning."

"I'm functioning."

"Are you? Ned's the only thing you talk about, think about—"

"Oh, God!" She closed her eyes against him.

"Lois, we'll do whatever we can. We'll keep the channels open and perhaps he'll come around. But if he doesn't, there's nothing more we can do. You have to face reality—"

"Reality? The reality is that if you'd shown the slightest bit of understanding—"

"You're saying it's *my* fault? Last I heard, it was Karen's fault for breaking up with him."

"I'm saying it ought to bother you that your son's floating around in limbo—"

"Of course it bothers me!"

"Does it? You've simply washed your hands—"

"All right!" He sat back in his chair with a violent movement. "Tell me, what more can I do? God knows I've tried. We've talked to Dr. Lyman. We've gone up there, we've talked to Ned, to Karen. In heaven's name, what else—"

"I'm really sorry you had to go to all that trouble!"

"Lois, you only make things worse by—"

"How could they be worse?" she screamed.

He looked horrified. "You'll drive yourself mad if you go on like this. Me, too, if I let you. And Amy. Why do you think Amy wanted to go away to school?"

"Is it mad to want to save Ned?" She pressed her trembling hands together.

"Lois, he knows where we are if he wants our help. You heard what Dr. Lyman said—it's up to Ned."

"You'll let him go by default, then? You simply don't care?"

"Of course I care!"

"Then act as though you care! Don't just—"

He stood up and walked out.

Seconds later she heard him drive away. Going where? To see a friend? A very private man, Gordon, not likely to confide in a friend about a personal problem. Another woman? She felt instinctively that that wasn't so. No, she knew where he'd gone—to his office at school, to work on his book. *Progressivism and the American Identity in the Nineteenth Century.* The nineteenth century held more interest for him than the contemporary scene that was their lives. But there was no use pressing him further. Once Gordon made up his mind, there was no changing him. He was firm and steady as a rock, a quality she had once admired. But like a rock, he wouldn't yield.

Well, neither would she, on this. She couldn't understand his attitude. She couldn't forgive the fact that he didn't seem to share or understand her anguish.

Since then she had largely given up talking to Gordon about Ned. She had stopped going to see Dr. Lyman, too, since he and Gordon seemed to be in league against her. In any case, she didn't like the direction Dr. Lyman had been taking lately, the things he seemed to be intimating about Ned. What on earth could he know about Ned anyway? Ned hadn't ever been his patient.

So now she kept her feelings mostly to herself. And outwardly her life with Gordon resumed its former even tenor. But inwardly her bitterness continued as she went on worrying, going over it all again and again, from the very beginning, or what seemed the beginning—that call from Ned last year saying he and Karen had broken up.

As his mother she ought to have recognized right from the start that something was terribly wrong. She had realized, of course, that Ned was upset, even distraught, and she certainly understood his distress. He and Karen had been going together for years, after all, and had been living together for a while in an apartment off campus. So it must have been traumatic, tearing apart two lives that had meshed. Still, people broke up all the time, especially at that age; they might feel lonely and unhappy for a while, but they got over it eventually, they didn't go completely to pieces.

It was like firing pots in the kiln, she thought. Some came whole through the test of fire, while others, because of some undetected flaw, cracked and broke.

. . .

When Fay died, Lois felt she had lost not only her mother but also an ally in the struggle to save Ned. When the trouble first started, Fay had joined Lois in trying to talk to Ned. She had gone with Lois to visit him in that college town where he'd stayed on though he'd stopped going to classes. Karen was still going to school and still living in the apartment she and Ned had shared. Karen told Lois that she'd offered Ned the apartment when they broke up, but he had said she could keep it, he would find somewhere else to live.

"Somewhere" amounted to nowhere, so far as Lois could tell. On her visits she always met Ned in some place he designated, some park or café. The addresses and phone numbers he supplied all seemed to belong to other people. Whenever she called to say she was coming, it was clear he wasn't living there, wherever. Yes, sure, she could leave a message, the voice on the telephone would say; Ned would get the message when he next stopped by. Sometimes the voice said "when," and sometimes "if." Once when she asked, "Who is this? Where am I calling?" the voice said brusquely, "This is Ron's place."

"Are you Ron?"

"No, I'm Vic." Or Al or Bob or Susie.

She'd mentioned this to Gordon back when they were still talking about Ned. "I don't understand how he's living. How he's getting by."

"Panhandling," Gordon said tersely. "Or drugs."

"Drugs? He doesn't seem—"

"How else? He's not working. We're not supporting him. You're not giving him money, are you?"

"Not enough to make any difference."

She'd agreed all along that they shouldn't support him or in any way make it easy for him to continue in this fashion. If Ned wouldn't go to school, he must work—at something, anything, painting houses, waiting tables, driving a truck, whatever. Still, it was agonizing to think of Ned as penniless, homeless. When she went to see him, she always left him a little cash, twenty dollars or so. He never asked for more, never asked for money at all. So perhaps Gordon was right; perhaps he was supporting himself through drugs.

The last time Fay had gone along to see Ned, it was obvious that her words were having no effect. As they'd driven home later, Lois had burst into tears. She'd had to pull over until she calmed down. Fay hugged her as she wept, held her tight, a solid presence. "Yes, baby, cry," she murmured. "Let it out, you'll feel better."

After Fay had her stroke, Lois tried calling Ned. She left message after message, and wrote him, too, asking him to come to see Fay. When Fay died, Lois again telephoned and wrote, asking if he'd come to the funeral.

Two days after the funeral, he finally called back, weeping. "I'm sorry," he kept saying. "Sorry, sorry . . ." Then he hung up.

Diane had gone to see him once. Probably at Fay's suggestion, Lois thought. Diane had rented a car and driven up one weekend. Nothing came of it, of course. Which was hardly surprising. How could Diane, of all people, who'd never even had children of her own, succeed where everyone else had failed?

Desperate, Lois had tried one final gambit: without telling Gordon, she had taken Amy to see Ned. She had coached Amy thoroughly in what to say and how to say it. When they arrived, she made a point of leaving Amy alone with Ned for a while. But when Lois rejoined them, there was no indication that anything had changed. And when she questioned Amy in the car afterward, Amy turned stone-silent and refused to answer.

•   •   •

As they sat down to dinner, Gordon recounted what had happened at the meeting. The meeting was about a colleague, Jim Bloom-field, over whose promotion dissension had arisen.

"As of now," Gordon said, "he won't get that promotion. He may even be out of a job at the end of the term."

Lois put food on his plate. "Doesn't anyone support him?"

"Only me," Gordon said. "Ironic, isn't it?"

It was, because Gordon hadn't been in favor of hiring Jim initially. She passed the plate over.

Gordon picked up his fork, then put it down again. "That's too much, Lois." His voice was suddenly querulous. "I can't eat that much, you know I can't." He passed the plate back.

She removed a chop. "All right?"

He nodded. "Peter Black brought up the question of grants. As if grants really had anything to do with it, as he very well knows. Then Viola joined in, and then Arnold. They keep saying he hasn't been effective, but precisely how he's fallen short, they can't seem to explain. . . ."

All her bitterness welled up as he continued. He'd been en-grossed for weeks in this problem of Jim's, but he wouldn't help with the problem of the one person in the world who, with Amy, meant most to them. And she was supposed to sit here and show interest. And now, today, on top of it all—

"Gordon."

At her tone he stopped in mid-sentence.

She told him about the afternoon's developments, taking care to keep her manner calm, her voice modulated. About this, any-way, he wouldn't be able to claim that she was ranting, irrational.

He looked incredulous. "You mean, he appeared at the door? Just like that?"

"Just like that."

"Why? What does he want?"

"Whatever, I'm not about to give it to him." She reached for the coffeepot.

"Well—I'm sorry. It must have been quite a shock. And here I've been running on about—"

She thought, That's the first understanding thing he's said in months.

"Where is he now?"

"At the house." She filled his cup, passed it to him. "Diane's letting him stay there tonight. Unbelievable, isn't she?"

Gordon gave her an odd look. "What's he like?"

"Like?" Her voice rose. "Who cares what he's like?"

"Well, I'm curious. He's your father, after all."

She laughed, shortly. "A pity it took him so long to remember that fact." She set the pot down. "Men seem to find it terribly easy to abandon their children."

Gordon flushed a dull red. He opened his mouth as though to speak, but it was her turn now to remove herself. She walked out of the room, out of the house, and drove to the Shed.

CHAPTER 4 . . .

After dinner, Diane and Charlie sat in the living room, talking, though *talk* was hardly the word for this dialogue that proceeded by stops and starts, filled with silent questions along with the spoken ones. For Diane's part, the pauses allowed for mental debates on how much to reveal in this or that answer. For his part—who knew?

"Have you lived out west all this time?"

"Yes." Pause. "Except at the beginning, when I . . . at the beginning." Pause. "You don't live here? In Shelburne?"

"No." Pause. "I live in New York City."

As though oil had been applied to a rusted mechanism, their talk grew a little easier as the evening progressed. With their words they seemed to offer each other beginning clues, as though setting in place the first pieces of a jigsaw puzzle. So far the pieces didn't add up to even the smallest part of a picture. They'd have a long way to go before that could happen.

"What do you do?"

"Well—" Why did she always preface this answer with *Well?* "I'm a free-lance writer. I write annual reports, company histories, that sort of thing." Pause. "And you?"

"Well—"

Perhaps it came from a kind of diffidence?

"—I'm a sort of . . . hotelkeeper."

"Oh. You've given up music then?"

"Given up?"

"I thought you played the piano. Professionally."

"Yes. Not as much as I used to, though." He didn't elaborate.

It sounded as though Lois's estimate wasn't too far off the mark: there was less and less work for an aging musician, so he'd had to turn to something else. Hotelkeeper. Manager? Or—she suddenly saw him as the desk clerk in a small, slightly seedy establishment, a lobby with a few shabby chairs in which men huddled in winy slumber.

Seated on the piano bench, Ella watched intently, her gaze turning from one to the other as they talked. Her attitude to Charlie seemed to change from minute to minute. When Diane had gone to put out bed linens for him in the room that had been Lois's, Ella had followed her in, and for a moment Diane thought she was going to make up his bed, but she only followed Diane out in silence. For dinner Diane had put together whatever was in the refrigerator—hamburger, leftover rice, salad. Did Ella want to make her specialty, carrots with orange? *No!* Ella shouted at the top of her voice, and shook her head so hard that Diane was afraid she would hurt herself. But minutes later she pulled a bowl noisily out of the cupboard and assembled flour, butter, sugar, and canned peaches to make dessert. She didn't speak to Charlie during the meal. Whenever he addressed her, she only stared at him open-mouthed, as though he were some exotic species. When he complimented her on the dessert—"This brown Betty is delicious, Ella"—she leaned across the table, stuck her face in his, and shrieked, "Cobbler, silly! Cobbler! Cobbler!"

"Stop that, Ella," Diane said firmly.

Ella stopped but muttered resentfully beneath her breath for the rest of the meal.

Yet when Diane suggested to Charlie after dinner that they

move to the living room, Ella went with them. This was the first time since Fay's death that she hadn't gone right upstairs to the rocking chair after dinner.

•   •   •

"Where did you go when you first . . . left?"

"New York." Pause. "I knew a few people there, musicians. I thought I could pick up some work. . . ."

While he talked, she studied him. There they were, the signs she'd once searched for in the mirror; his nose was wider than hers at the bridge but had the same sharp tip; her pale coloring was his, and her eyes had a downward slope like his at the outer corners. (Panda eyes, Adam said.) Something else she noticed, too, as he made that gesture, raising his hand absently to his earlobe: each lobe had a slight natural depression, a slight dimple. So did hers, and Ella's.

". . . After a while, I joined a trio going west on tour. Their piano player had gotten sick. We worked together as far as Chicago. . . ."

He was studying her, too, she noticed. And Ella. Superficially Ella looked like no one else in the family, except that her large hands with prominent knuckles were distinctly Fay's. But Ella was double-jointed; there was a trick that only she could do, bending her thumbs all the way back. Diane repressed the impulse to ask Charlie whether he could do that.

"And then?"

"Then?" He gazed into the fireplace, where logs burned desultorily. " 'Then' is a very long story."

Diane had lit the fire because the room seemed oddly bleak and cheerless. Too large. Earlier the sound of rain had helped fill in the silences, smooth over the awkwardness. But the rain had stopped, and now she seemed to feel, palpably, the aura of another presence. It was only to be expected, of course, in this house still filled with signs and echoes of Fay.

Thinking of Fay, she grew more and more uneasy. What would

her mother have thought if she'd known who was here, in this room, this house? If she could see Diane chatting with him as though he were anyone at all, an acquaintance, a friend?

Forgive me.

As though in answer, the clock in the hall began to chime. Diane jumped as though caught in some obscene act. That clock, a schoolhouse clock made of burled walnut, had been a particular treasure of Fay's. Ella, too, loved it; she always stopped whatever she was doing to count off its chimes, moving her lips silently. "Nine!" she pronounced now, importantly.

Glancing at Charlie, Diane saw that he, too, was listening. For him, too, it seemed, this was the sound of memory.

"Was the clock here when—"

"Yes. As a matter of fact, I bought it for Fay. On our third anniversary."

Was it true? Why not? Why would he invent such a thing? But suddenly she seemed to hear Lois's voice, scornful. *Presenting himself as a fond husband.*

He patted his pockets, then began to get up. "I've left my cigarettes—"

"I have some." She offered them.

"Thank you." He took one, lit it. "I'm sorry to see we have this in common."

She shrugged. "I'm trying to cut down."

He inhaled, then exhaled slowly. "I stopped once. For a year."

"Cold turkey?"

He nodded. "It was . . . kind of a deal. To appease Fate, or whatever."

"Fate wasn't appeased?"

"Something like that." She saw him consciously decide to change the subject. "When do you have to move? From here, I mean."

Why was he asking? Should she tell him?

Suddenly Ella swung around on the bench and began to pound

the keys with both hands. The clamor set Diane's teeth on edge. "Ella, please!"

Ella went on pounding. But when Charlie went and sat on the bench beside her, she stopped abruptly, hands in midair.

"Watch, Ella." He spread his right hand and played a chord. "Like this." He played it again. "Now you do it." Ella only gazed, her mouth ajar.

Like a summons from a distant planet, the telephone rang. Diane hurried to answer. It was Mario.

She apologized for not having called back.

"That's all right. Nothing urgent." He sounded downcast.

This was the first time they had spoken since the funeral, where, to Lois's annoyance, he had wept freely, audibly.

"Quite a display," Lois had commented afterward.

"It's no crime to show feeling, Lois. Mother was the same, she didn't hold back."

"Don't I know!"

"Personally," Diane had said, "I'm glad Mother had someone like Mario. He was good for her, made her happy. I only wish she had met him sooner. . . ."

"I've been thinking about you," Diane told him now. "How are you feeling?"

"Lousy. God, I miss her. She was one terrific woman, your mother. Full of life, always ready to laugh. We had the best times—" He broke off.

He had called to ask a favor. He had some snapshots of Fay, but they were small, nothing special. He would like a good photograph, something larger, if possible. Did Diane by any chance have one she could spare?

At first she couldn't think of anything. But then she remembered one she'd always liked.

"There *is* one, if I can find it, though it's not very recent. But it's a good shot." The picture had been taken some years back for a business mailer.

She would look for it, she said.

Mario told her he had driven by the house and seen the SOLD sign.

"You should have come in."

"I thought of it, but, well . . ."

Was it that he couldn't bear to be in the house, with Fay gone? Or had he seen Lois's car and felt he wouldn't be welcome? He probably knew how Lois felt about him. Probably mutual, she thought. Oil and water, those two.

He sounded so despondent that for a moment she thought of inviting him over. They could talk about Fay. It might help him. Help both of them. Not now, though, with Charlie there. Perhaps over the weekend.

When she suggested it, Mario said he was going away for the weekend, to New York. His son, Phil, had just become a father, and he wanted to see his new grandson. He would take in some music, too; they were doing *Tosca* at the Met. He wouldn't be back until Monday afternoon. The shop was closed Mondays, so the weekend was a good time to get away. And there was nothing to hurry back for now, he said sadly.

"Monday evening, then. Come and have a drink. I may have found that photo by then."

He accepted, sounding grateful. How were things going at the house? Was there anything he could do, any help they needed? He'd be glad to help with the move.

Oh, God—moving. She didn't want to think about it, all the work entailed and, even worse, prying Ella out. Though she herself hadn't lived in the house for years, leaving it was going to be a wrenching experience. If *she* felt that way, how could they expect Ella to go quietly?

She hung up and went back to the living room. Charlie was playing a bluesy lament. Ella, seated beside him, was obviously enthralled.

Diane sat down, listening. The music was familiar, though she couldn't remember the title. Adam liked jazz. She had been going with him to clubs this past year, and somewhere she had heard this. Her mind held the image of a chunky black woman whose voice had a wonderful sandpaper edge. "Trouble is a man . . ." That was it. ". . . A man who loves me no more, no more. Trouble is a man, a man I'll always adore. . . ."

One night, soon after they'd met, Adam had taken her to some place in the Village—Bradley's, was it?—to hear a pianist he especially liked. She couldn't remember who it was, though she did remember the way he'd sounded, the way he'd looked, with his head bent so low it almost touched the keyboard. That night she had told Adam about her father.

"A piano player? Jazz?" He seemed delighted.

"Classically trained, but he plays—played—jazz on the side."

"Is he good?"

"I've no idea. He was gone before I ever knew him."

"Do you miss him? The idea of him?"

She shrugged. "You can't miss what you haven't known."

Now she sat listening, watching, as Charlie filled the room with music. All these years, and now here he was, alive, tangible.

Forgive me, Mother, I have to know him.

The last notes faded.

"More, more!" Ella crowed, exactly as when Fay used to play.

"Tomorrow, Ella."

She stamped her foot. "Now!"

"I'm tired, Ella." Charlie stood up.

Unexpectedly Ella turned docile. "Okey-dokey," she said—an expression she'd picked up from some television program. She left abruptly, in her usual way, with no preamble or good-night.

Minutes later the sound of rocking began.

Charlie looked startled. "What's that?"

Diane explained. One thing led to another, and soon she was telling him about Ella and how Fay's death had left her especially bereft.

He looked thoughtful. "What will happen to Ella now? Is there some plan—?"

She told him what Lois had proposed.

"That'll be a radical change for her, won't it?"

Did she detect a critical note? From *him?* "Anything at all will be a radical change," she said, coolly. "We're not exactly beset with choices."

Again, the telephone rang. As she went to answer, she wondered for a second whether it might be Adam. He wasn't due back in the country till the end of next week, but—

"Diane? This is Jake. How're you doing?"

Oh. "All right, thanks, Jake. What's up?"

As always, he came right to the point.

"I hate like hell to bother you, but are you likely to be available soon? Kandex wants a company history."

"Sorry, Jake, I'd like to do it, but—"

"They specifically asked for you, Diane. They liked the report you did last year."

"Are they in a hurry?"

"Yep. Printed by the end of December."

"What's the rush?"

"It's for their centennial. They're firm about the date, and I'm not about to argue."

Jake worked for a large printing company that hired free-lancers to write some of what it printed. Kandex was a major account, a sizable feather in Jake's cap. She could understand his wanting to keep them happy. And from her own point of view, it made sense to accommodate Jake as much as possible.

"You wouldn't have to be gone very long. Not at this stage. Just a quick trip to Cleveland, two days, that's all, do the interviews, collect the material. You can work on it at home. We'll take care of graphics later."

Two days. Lois wouldn't be pleased.

"Diane, you know this is important to me."

"When would I have to be there?"

"Monday, early. Better if you could leave Sunday, be in Frank Vigo's office first thing Monday."

On the other hand, two days were no big deal. Lois could surely take over for just two days.

She told him she'd do it. Then something occurred to her. "I don't have the right clothes with me."

Jake told her to buy what she needed in Shelburne and add it to the bill.

They discussed travel arrangements. He'd make them, as usual, book flights, a hotel. He'd call back with the details.

She returned to the living room and found it empty. Charlie had placed the screen around the fireplace and gone upstairs. She could hear him moving around in the room that had been Lois's. She felt cheated; there was so much more she still wanted to ask him. Tomorrow, then. Before he left.

On her way to bed, she looked in Fay's room to check on Ella. Ella sometimes fell asleep in the rocking chair and had to be woken and gotten to bed. But tonight she lay beneath the bedclothes, snoring gently.

In bed later, Diane lay awake, conjecturing. Watching Charlie tonight, she had tried to picture what would have attracted Fay all those years before. But any image of youth, strength, or sexual attraction was overwhelmed by the present reality of this aging man, who seemed faded and frail compared with Fay. Still, he was certainly intelligent and confident; he had probably been quite personable once.

Supposing he'd returned while Fay was alive? She tried to imagine them together, but the picture eluded her—partly because she couldn't see Fay as half of a married couple. Fay seemed too individual to be the mere half of any twosome. Of course, it was true that she had only ever known her mother as single, a woman on her own. But even after Fay had met Mario, she had still always seemed a single self-sufficient unit, with Mario a welcome addition but not an integral half.

Even as a younger man Charlie must have been very different from Mario. It was easy to understand the attraction of Mario. Lois looked down her nose, of course, but Lois had always been disposed to find fault with Fay, no matter what she did. And Lois was obviously uncomfortable with the idea that her mother might still have wanted or enjoyed a sexual relationship. It had been all very well for Fay to proclaim, over and over, that she had no use for men and to warn her daughters never to trust them or rely on them, men brought nothing but grief. It was nevertheless always clear that Fay was still interested in sex, though she often seemed impatient with herself for wanting—needing—a sexual life. She seemed to think it would be better if she could eliminate that need, cut desire out of her as though with a scalpel.

How she had bloomed after meeting Mario. . . .

It had been clear from the start that it was the physical side of the relationship that meant the most to Fay. That was obviously important to Mario, too, of course, but in addition, Mario had been in love with Fay in a way that she probably hadn't returned, Diane thought. Fay had declared frequently that she would never fall in love again.

"Take what you want from a man, and leave it at that," she'd told Diane. "You'll be better off, believe me."

"You sound," Diane retorted, "like the kind of man who only thinks of women as sexual objects."

Fay shrugged. "It's the only way you'll come through unscathed. Take it from one who knows."

• • •

Diane fell asleep and dreamed that Adam was with her. They moved together till her flesh seemed to melt; her body became a warm, thick liquid flowing over countless thresholds, and she cried out harshly, as though in pain instead of pleasure.

She woke and lay staring into the darkness, wanting a cigarette, thinking of Adam.

· · ·

Lois called the next morning to say she had made an appointment for Ella at the center, for nine-thirty on Monday. "I spoke to a Mrs. Corry there. She was very helpful."

Diane's heart sank. "Monday?"

"What's wrong with Monday?"

"Something's come up. I have to go to Cleveland. . . ." She explained about the job.

"What about Ella, while you're gone?"

"Can't you stay here, just for two days?"

"We have houseguests arriving Sunday afternoon."

"Couldn't Gordon take them out to dinner?"

"It's not just anyone, it's Leonard Bayer. He's coming to give the Dryden lecture. Hilda will be with him."

"I thought we were supposed to help each other."

"You're certainly being a lot of help, dashing off at the first opportunity. You know very well Ella won't go without you."

"Can you change the appointment?"

"The only way I got an appointment this week was because someone canceled out for Monday. I don't want to delay it another full week."

Gridlock. Now what? "I've already said I'd go to Cleveland, Lois. Where does that leave us?"

"Leave me, you mean. You've left me no choice, obviously. I'll have to stay over there while you're gone. But you'll have to persuade Ella to go with me to the center."

"I'll talk to her as soon as she gets back."

"Back?"

"She's gone for a walk. With Charlie."

"A walk? Ella?" Lois sounded incredulous, as well she might.

Diane recounted how she had come downstairs at seven o'clock to find Ella, who normally had to be roused out of bed, already up and dressed. In her best dress, in fact, a blue shirtwaist with brass buttons. Charlie had gotten up early, too. Ella had cooked them a splendid breakfast. "Last night she stayed downstairs until ten."

There was a brief silence.

"Doesn't any of this strike you as odd?" Lois demanded.

"In a way, yes. But aren't you glad? For Ella?"

"I guess so," Lois said grudgingly. "But you surely don't expect me to be grateful? To *him*?"

•   •   •

Persuading Ella was easier said than done. Diane had hardly started before Ella shook her head vigorously.

"But, Ella, you haven't even heard—"

Ella clapped her hands over her ears.

Charlie stayed quiet, listening, watching.

"Ella, listen . . ." Carefully, Diane explained, keeping it simple: the lady at the center knew what a good cook Ella was; she wanted to talk to her; she might be able to find her a job doing cooking; Ella would be paid wages for cooking because she was good at it; there would be other people there, Ella would have friends. . . .

Ella stared blankly, showing no interest.

Diane's hopes ebbed. What, after all, could "job" mean to Ella, who had never held a job? What could "wages" mean to Ella, who had never spent any money on her own? What could "friends" mean to Ella, under the circumstances?

"You see, Ella—"

"*No!*" Ella's eyes were suddenly slitted. She picked up a coffee mug and banged it down hard on the counter.

Charlie moved forward. "Where is the center, exactly?"

Diane told him.

"That's near Brookfield Gardens, isn't it? The greenhouse? Is it still there?"

She nodded.

He turned to Ella. "Have you been to Brookfield, Ella?"

Ella looked at Diane for an answer.

"Where they grow the flowers, Ella. We used to go there with Mother, remember? When we were children."

"Tell you what, Ella," Charlie said. "We'll go see the lady about the cooking. After that, we'll go see the flowers."

Ella stared. After a moment she said cautiously, "You come?"

"Yes. We'll go in my car. Remember I showed you how the roof slides open? If it's warm, we'll open the roof."

So he knew Brookfield. Had he gone there with them a life-time ago, one of those fathers you saw on a Sunday outing, walking along with a wife, family, holding a child by the hand, pushing an infant in a stroller down the walkway between the resplendent blossoms?

Ella remained impassive. Then she looked at Diane. "You come?"

"I can't, Ella, I'm sorry. But Lois will."

Ella's expression remained unchanged. Diane held her breath. Then, to her relief, she saw Ella nod.

It took her a moment to realize: this meant Charlie would have to stay through Monday.

· · ·

When she called Lois back to report what had happened, Lois sounded outraged. "You mean you're going to let him stay on?"

"Lois, we need him for this. Ella wouldn't have agreed without him. What's more, I don't think you'll have to move over here. He can keep an eye—"

"You mean you'd actually consider leaving him alone there?" She was almost shouting.

"D'you think he'll run off with the silver?"

"Very funny! I'll certainly stay at the house while you're gone. And *I'll* take Ella to the center."

"I doubt she'll go without him."

"All right, he can come along, too, if she insists."

"Lois, he seems willing to take some responsibility. I should think you'd be glad—"

"Better late than never, you mean? That doesn't cut much ice. When will you be back?"

"Tuesday night."

Partly because she was genuinely curious, and partly to divert Lois from her anger, Diane asked what Gordon thought about Charlie's return.

"He thinks what I think," Lois answered, a little too quickly. "That he's got something up his sleeve. An eye to the main chance."

"Main chance of what?"

"Isn't it obvious? He's already got a foothold. A roof over his head."

"Not for long."

"We'll see," Lois said grimly.

"For heaven's sake, Lois, must you always swim upstream?"

"Must you always take the easy way out?" Lois retorted.

Just as well she was getting away for a while, albeit to work, Diane thought. She could use a respite from family tensions. Away, she'd be able to think more clearly, get some perspective.

Not only about Charlie. She was going to have to decide what to do about Adam.

CHAPTER 5 • • •

Moonlight slanting in the window showed regiments of rosebuds marching diagonally across the wallpaper. Lying there, Charlie tried to picture Lois in this room, Lois as a young girl, surrounded by rosebuds. It was difficult to picture Lois as a teenager, with youthful habits of inquiry or eagerness. Difficult to match her with the round, rosy-cheeked infant who, at one year, had pulled herself up to a standing position by holding on to his leg as he'd sat at the piano, or with the sober-faced child whose dark eyes had followed him constantly.

He turned over, moving carefully, trying to find a better position for his shoulder. Pain radiated to the top of his arm, making him wince. Bursitis. Days, it was tolerable. It was at night, as he lay awake, that he really felt it. If it didn't ease up soon, he'd get up and take a pill. He would have to get up soon, anyway. Hard to say which was worse about age—the threat of mortality itself or the demands and indignities of a weak bladder, loss of teeth and hair, failing eyesight.

Tonight Ella was rocking. It sounded quieter up here than it did from below, but it was still disturbing. Out of the cradle, endlessly rocking . . .

Yesterday, as they'd walked together around the block, she had taken his hand. A strange pair they must seem, he'd thought, this great, galumphing girl and himself. Girl, yes, never mind her age. Not a line on that face with its flattened expression. Tabula rasa, an innocent. She didn't speak as they walked, but now and then she glanced at him sideways, with her lopsided, uncertain smile. When he smiled back, she put her hand over her mouth, in that way of hers, and ducked her head. Physically she reminded him a little of his father. The same gauntness and that tall, strong-looking build.

Lois, on the other hand, so much resembled Fay that he'd have known who she was no matter where they had met. When she was younger, she must have been Fay's double. But she lacked Fay's spark, liveliness, sexuality—whatever the combination was that had drawn him irresistibly to Fay the moment he'd first laid eyes on her. What a time that was, at Chautauqua, in that bucolic setting, with the crowds, the music, the green dazzle of summer. One Saturday night, after he'd played a concert in the afternoon, he and Fay had gone dancing. Fay loved to dance; she was light on her feet, though you wouldn't have thought it, substantial as she was, wide at the shoulders, broad at the hips—very much a woman, with that ripe body, thick dark hair, high color.

Diane looked nothing like Fay. In appearance, she reminded him of Jeanette. Nettie. Dead of meningitis when she was fourteen and he sixteen. Too bad his parents hadn't known Diane; it would have been like Nettie coming back to them.

His parents had been shocked when he left. They had told him so in no uncertain terms, on the few occasions he'd called. They had tried to keep in touch with Fay, chiefly because of the children. But even though they were on her side, Fay had refused to have any more to do with them. She wrote them saying she was severing all ties with anyone connected with him. She had kept her word. A hard woman. And unfair, penalizing them for his actions. What had his parents ever done to her? But fairness had never been Fay's strong point.

Strong. There was the word. She was strong, yes, always sure of herself, always sure she was right. She had no doubts, ever. That strength, that certainty used to scare him. Not at first, though. At first everything had seemed perfect, as it always does when you're deeply in love. They'd become lovers the second time they met. Fay was the only woman he'd ever known back then who went to bed as naturally and wholeheartedly as someone else might give you a hug. Because of that, he'd been surprised to find she was still a virgin. In bed she was everything a man could want. And at first she was pleased with him, too, he could tell. But that went to pieces later, of course, when their differences began.

The thing was—it took him years to understand this—Fay had had an image of him, right from the start, that he couldn't have lived up to even if he'd wanted. She had been determined to make him fit that image, like it or not.

Part of the problem had to do with her own history. The other part was what he himself had seemed to her when they met. That summer he'd been playing with the Chautauqua Symphony. And his regular job in those days was still with the opera company. At that point he hadn't yet realized he was in transition. So when he later decided he wanted to do something else, be something else, Fay felt she had been deceived.

He should have been more cautious. He should have listened more carefully right from the start, from the very beginning. He should have been more alert not just to Fay's words but to what was really meant by those words, and what they might mean for the future. But who, wrapped in the throes of sexual ardor, bothers with words and their true significance? He hadn't. Nor, for that matter, had she.

They had shared stories of their respective childhoods. He didn't see his as especially burdensome, except for one thing: after

Nettie had died, his parents had made it clear that since he had survived and Nettie had not, he owed it to them to make up for this loss; the least he could do was fulfill the dream his mother had for him.

His father, a dour and parsimonious man, was a minor railroad official in St. Louis. His mother played the organ at church and taught piano to children who came to the house for weekly lessons. Nettie and he grew up hearing Stephen Foster songs and Sousa marches picked out with varying degrees of proficiency on the upright piano in the enclosed sun porch, which his mother called "the studio." Naturally he and Nettie were started on piano in first grade.

His parents were strict Baptists, and the household was rigidly structured in all respects, from church attendance to chores to mealtimes. He might have rebelled against the additional demands of piano practice if he hadn't enjoyed the outlet that music brought, the only outlet allowed in that house. Because he persevered, his mother began to entertain visions of him as a future concert star. At twelve, despite his father's objections to the cost, he was sent to a local music school. At seventeen, he won a scholarship to the Cincinnati Conservatory.

"You're all we have now," his father said the day he left. "Make sure we'll have reason to be proud of you." He laid a hand weightily on his son's shoulder. His mother's eyes were swollen from weeping at his imminent departure. Her lips touched his cheek like the dry flutter of a moth. She surreptitiously pressed into his hand a small, oval-framed photograph of Nettie.

In Cincinnati he soon found out where he really stood. Still, he got through his time there all right, though with no particular distinction. Not knowing quite what he wanted to do next, he went on to the Boston Conservatory to get a master's degree in piano and theory. After that he taught for a while, first at a music school on the North Shore, then at a small college in western Massachusetts. But he really didn't like full-time teaching, so he looked around for something else. Finally he took a job as staff accompanist with the orchestra of a newly formed opera company in Shelburne. The salary wasn't anything to write home about, but on the side he did some free-lance accompanying, took on private students, and found additional work when he could at other schools and festivals.

Then, quite by chance, he began to get into another kind of music. It started when he and Sy Merkel got talking.

Sy Merkel played timpani in the opera orchestra, and moon-lighted with his own band, Merk's Music Makers, at dances and weddings. Sy was in his fifties, the oldest member of the orchestra. He was divorced, lived alone, and was inclined to be testy; there wasn't much social exchange between him and the others. But one day, after a rehearsal, Charlie started noodling on the piano, and Sy came over.

" 'April in Paris,' huh? You play jazz, Charlie?"

No, Charlie said, he didn't know the first thing about jazz, but he'd started listening to songs lately, popular music.

"There's a piano player coming to town does 'April in Paris' like nothing you ever heard. Bud Powell, bop player. Used to play with Cootie Williams. Man's got emotional problems, but, boy, can he play. I'm going to catch him Friday night. Want to come along?"

They were doing *Carmen* Friday night, Charlie reminded him.

"We'll be through in time to catch the last couple sets. You should hear this guy, Charlie. One of the all-time greats."

Struck by Sy's uncharacteristic enthusiasm, Charlie said he'd go along.

The club was located next to a brewery, in a tiny basement where the cigarette smoke hung like a pall between the listeners and the man at the piano. The cash register was so loud it almost drowned out the music. The piano player seemed lost in some awful darkness of his own. But what Charlie heard that night lodged in his head forever. He went to Sy's place afterward to listen to records, while Sy talked on and on about Powell, his right hand, his upbeat tempo, those incredible strings of eighth notes. . . .

When Sy talked like this, he seemed a different person. Char-lie felt as though he himself, too, had somehow been transformed, set on fire by that music, and he burned to hear more, know more. He couldn't remember ever feeling this way about classical music. Lately, in fact, he seemed to be going through some kind of slump. He was still playing and teaching, but he was finding it more and more difficult to summon up real interest. He no longer partici-pated in all the talk about performances and playing. He did very little practicing. He was doing only what was minimally necessary to get by.

. . .

From then on he started listening to jazz wherever he could find it—recordings, radio, live performances. He listened to pianists— Bud Powell, of course, and Fats Waller, Teddy Wilson, Art Tatum. He listened to bands—Basie, Chick Webb, Ellington.

One night Sy's piano player came down sick, and Sy asked Charlie if he'd like to fill in. All Charlie could play at that point were simple chords and fragments of melody, so he didn't exactly jump at the idea. But Sy seemed to think he'd do all right, so he finally agreed to try.

It turned out to be a mixed experience. He enjoyed it, but he had trouble keeping up, and he played all the bridges wrong. He apologized to Sy afterward, feeling he had let him down.

"Don't worry about it. It wasn't that bad," Sy told him. "Next time you'll do better."

"I've been thinking," Charlie said. "I'd like to get some in-struction. Any ideas?"

Sy told him about a piano player named Jackie Lee Peartree, who lived above an appliance store on Egmont Street, across the river. "Came out of Kansas City, used to play with Cab Calloway.

About eighty years old, but the guy's got chops. Look him up, why
don't you?"

Charlie looked him up.

Jackie Lee Peartree studied him dubiously over glasses mended
with cellophane tape. "You been playin' on the beat for a good
while now. Think you can learn to play 'round it instead?"

"I'd like to try," Charlie said.

"Hand me that cane." Slowly he made his way across the room
to the piano.

After that, Charlie went to see Jackie Lee twice a week. Those
hours spent in that shabby room over the store became the focal
point of his existence. Whenever he had any time to spare—an
afternoon, an hour, ten minutes—he sat down and practiced this
music that was joyous and dark, hot and cool, loving and celebra-
tory. Exciting, filled with pleasurable tension. And something
else, too: after years of playing music note for note, the unstruc-
tured aspect of jazz was liberating; whenever he played, barriers
seemed to fall away that had kept him prisoner all his life. At first
the challenge of improvising made him nervous, but as he grew
used to it, the freedom to create his own rhythm and melodies was
heady.

· · ·

Soon he became the regular substitute in Sy's band, and then he
began to look for additional gigs with other bands. He played for
dances, weddings, parties, club dates. There weren't many clubs as
such around Shelburne, but there were quite a few bars, and many
of them had a piano, even if it was just an old upright with some
keys, hammers, or strings missing. Sometimes he could line up
solo gigs in these places. Most of these spots were fairly sleazy. "In
this business, you'll play in toilets before you're through," Sy told
him. Charlie didn't care. He liked the informality and lack of
pretension of jazz musicians and felt at home in their surroundings.

But when he'd first met Fay, all this had barely started. For Fay—and for him as well at that stage—he was still essentially what she thought he was, what he spent most of his time being: Charles Hazzard, classical pianist. (Always "Charles" to his parents and Fay, never "Charlie.")

•   •   •

As for Fay, her mother had died when she was five. Her father, who worked for an insurance company in Philadelphia, had done the best he could for a while, but when Fay was six, he sent her to be cared for by her mother's aunts. Lydia and Phoebe lived in Crowell, a small town in Pennsylvania. They were determined to do their duty by Fay, but there wasn't much for a child in the way of fun or companionship.

"I was lonely," Fay told Charlie. "There were no other children in the neighborhood. And I wasn't encouraged to bring friends home from school. Lydia wanted the house kept tidy, and Phoebe wanted peace and quiet when she got home from the shop. At their age, it was understandable, I suppose. But someday," she said, "I want a house filled with the sounds of voices and music and children."

It sounded wonderful, Charlie thought, moved.

Phoebe. Lydia. The names conjured up flowers pressed between the pages of a book of poems, but Fay's aunts didn't fit that picture. Their shop was called The Corsetarium, and both Phoebe and Lydia were firmly girded in its products. Phoebe, who mainly ran the shop, was briskly efficient, though when she relaxed with a glass of sherry at the end of the day, she became quite expansive. Lydia, short and stout, resembled pictures of Queen Victoria, though less severe. The house and meals were Lydia's main responsibility; she liked to cook and was an excellent baker.

Fay's father came to visit once a month. Whenever she saw him, Fay asked when she'd be going home, but he was always evasive. When she was seven, he remarried; his new wife was a widow. A month later Lydia and Phoebe told Fay she was at last going home; her father and stepmother would be coming to collect her the following week. Lydia wept a little, but Phoebe was sensible and forthright. At night Fay lay awake too excited to sleep.

On the specified day her father and his new wife turned up, accompanied by two children a little younger than Fay—her new stepbrother and stepsister. Consumed with jealousy at seeing these two with her father, Fay burst into tears and slapped their faces. By the time they all left her aunts' house, Fay wasn't exactly in favor with her new family. After a bad three months she was returned to Lydia and Phoebe's care.

Whenever her father visited after that, Fay begged him tearfully to take her with him. He always said uneasily that they must wait until she was a little older. She couldn't interrupt her schooling. And she didn't want to hurt her aunts' feelings, did she? They would miss her very much if she left them. She would surely miss them, too, wouldn't she?

As time passed, Fay began to realize this was true. She was used to Phoebe and Lydia by now, and the way they lived. The house, which had at first struck her as silent and gloomy, was home now, familiar; she felt settled there. Besides, Phoebe always had stories to tell about her customers at The Corsetarium. And Lydia was now teaching Fay to cook; she had come to enjoy working alongside her aunt in the fragrant warmth of the kitchen.

In addition, though her aunts didn't provide the standard amenities of a typically happy childhood, they had certain cultural interests. They belonged to a book circle which met in members' houses to discuss selected novels and biographies. And they were musical: Lydia had an uneven soprano and belonged to a choral group; Phoebe played the piano. Fay begged for dancing lessons, which she didn't get, but they started her on piano instruction when she was eight, and she took to it immediately. Those piano lessons made up for a great deal, she told Charlie.

As the months and years went by, her father's visits grew further and further apart. By the time she was fourteen, he was coming to see her three times a year. One of those occasions was usually her birthday.

A week before her fifteenth birthday, he collapsed with a heart attack and was rushed to the hospital. Despite Lydia and Phoebe's attempts to persuade her, Fay refused to go to see him. He died three weeks later.

After high school Fay went to Oberlin, where she majored in piano and music education. By the time she met Charlie, she had been teaching for six months at a community music school in Crowell.

. . .

They were married three months after they met.

At first everything was all right. More than all right. Why not? He did whatever she wanted. The opera company was about to disband, but there was a teaching position available at the Adler School in Shelburne. At Fay's urging, he applied for it and got it. They bought the house Fay chose, half the down payment coming from money her father had left her. And they started a family almost immediately. For a brief time after they married, Fay taught piano at a private school for girls in Shelburne, but she gave that up when she found she was pregnant and instead began giving lessons at home.

It seemed to Charlie, looking back, that Fay began to change as soon as their first child was born. Their whole way of living changed. He hadn't realized this would happen. Fay wouldn't allow him to play when the baby was sleeping, in case the sound disturbed her. And she wanted him to play only classical music; she seemed to think anything else would have a deleterious effect on the child. Of course, she herself didn't like any other kind of music. No, that wasn't quite true—she liked to dance, after all. The thing was, she didn't want *him* to play any other kind of music. Certainly not professionally. So when he ultimately formed his

own group and started playing on occasional evenings and weekends, she wasn't exactly pleased. He pointed out they could use the
extra money. But she said at once that he was only using money as
an excuse, that he really liked playing that trash, there was no use
denying it. He didn't deny it. Why should he? What was wrong
with it anyway?

She lost her temper and railed at him. How, with his background, his training, could he lower himself to that kind of
music? It wasn't just the music, either—it was the kind of people
who played it, and the kinds of places they played in. And the
hours! He was out half the night, playing in dives. And he was
never around anymore on weekends. She was leading the life of a
widow. And Lois would grow up hardly knowing her father. He
owed them more of his time, his life, himself. His teaching job
was enough time spent away. In any case, if he'd drop that rinky-
dink stuff and apply himself properly, he'd go further with his real
career.

His real career? That was nonsense, he said, and she knew it.
There was no point kidding themselves about that.

At this, she grew even more incensed. "Giving up before
you've even tried!" He was a fine pianist, a superb musician; how
could he so degrade his talent?

He stared at her. He wasn't and never would be superb; he was
adequate, that was all. He'd always known his limitations, he said.
Yet here she was, trying to pretend he was something he had never
been or claimed to be, in order to fit some fantasy of her own.

There was more to it than the music, of course. Music was only
the catalyst. He knew that, and so, he guessed, did she. There was
far more at stake here than the music.

•   •   •

Yet between all the disputes, a certain kind of feeling still existed
between them. On the rare occasions when Fay seemed to soften
or appeared willing to consider his point of view, he would reach

out to her again with some hope, some aching need that she seemed willing, even eager, to fill. When this happened, they would make love as freely, tenderly, and passionately as they had at the beginning. Of course, she had her hopes and needs, too. He knew that. For her sake, he wished he could be what she wanted, conform to what she wished him to be. But at the same time he clung tenaciously to his own evolving sense of self.

Things grew steadily worse. By the time Diane was born, he was playing as many gigs as he could. Between teaching and playing, he was out a great deal.

One night he came in at two o'clock after playing at Murphy's, a bar down by the river. He was still high on the music. There'd been a good crowd, more listeners than drunks, and the music had gone exceptionally well. There'd been no sense of the hours passing as one chorus led to another, the piano taking a solo, then the bass, then the drums, then exchanging fours, then playing the head again. From Murphy's, the others had gone over to the bass player's for a jam session. They wanted Charlie to go along, but he knew he'd better not. He wouldn't get home until dawn if he did, and that would mean trouble. He'd have liked to ask them to come to his place to jam, but Fay wouldn't take kindly to that.

As he came alone into the dark and silent house, he felt he had to play for a while or he would burst. But as soon as he sat down and struck the first notes, Fay appeared.

"The baby's just gone to sleep! You'll wake her!"

She looked exhausted and unkempt in her nightgown. She was still fairly heavy after Diane's birth, and much of the time a faint sour smell, which came from the baby's constant spitting up, hung about her. Diane was colicky and cried for hours on end. It was true that Fay had to spend hours rocking her, walking the floor with her, to get her to sleep. But he would play quietly. And he'd given up the chance to jam with the others. It didn't seem a lot to ask.

Within minutes they were fighting and Fay was reproaching

him. "It's not enough that you're never around! When you *are* here, you make life more difficult!"

At the sound of their raised, quarreling voices, Diane woke and started to cry the thin wail of a four-month-old. Soon Lois was joining in.

Fay went upstairs. She came back down carrying the baby, Lois trailing after her in her sleeper, rubbing her eyes with her knuckles as she followed her mother into the room.

"Your daughters," Fay said. "Look at them. You've hardly seen them since they were born! Isn't it time you realized you have some responsibilities? To them? To me?"

The baby had an undeniably waiflike appearance. Just now her woebegone face was screwed up with rage or colicky pain as she yowled. Her small fists belabored the air as Fay held her out, and Charlie took her and kissed her. Lois ran to him then, and he hugged her, too. Yet inwardly his resentment swelled because Fay was using the children to manipulate him, to get what she wanted. But he agreed to cut down on the number of jobs he played and to spend more time at home in the future. And Fay, given her way, became loving once more, and seemingly content.

For a while he kept his promise and played only on occasional weekends. But without the respite of gigs, he found it more and more difficult to apply himself to teaching. This wasn't the way he'd planned to spend his life, listening to student after student struggle through the Hanon exercises or give a lachrymose reading of a Chopin prelude.

By the time Diane was a year old, the situation had badly deteriorated. He was again booking as many jobs as he could get, and Fay seemed permanently enraged. He'd have liked to quit teaching entirely and devote himself full-time to jazz, but he knew that would strain matters to a breaking point. For one thing, he'd be out almost every night of the week, playing. For another, it would mean giving up a certain amount of financial security. Teaching, after all, was regular employment, with normal hours and other benefits, including what Fay thought of as status. More status, anyway, than for a piano player whose milieu consisted mostly of bars, clubs, and party houses.

When Fay told him she was again pregnant, he felt the end of the world had come. He couldn't even pretend to be pleased. She wept and said she wasn't feeling well, and there was so much to cope with, and she hardly ever saw him. She was sick of trying to deal with everything herself—not only the children but also the things that needed doing around the house that never got done because he was always out, playing. She needed him there, he must help out more . . . and on and on and on. . . .

He listened with a feeling of rising panic. Then he lost control. If she had so damn much to do, it was because she had chosen it, he shouted. God knows *he* hadn't wanted three children. And she had put this last pregnancy over on him. What the hell had she done with her diaphragm, anyway, put it in a rummage sale?

He saw her watching him, gauging—he thought—when to weep harder, when to bring the children onto the scene. He felt no love for her now, and no pity. On the contrary, he felt active dislike for this woman who had lost not only her bright good looks but the zest and gaiety that had so attracted him, and who now whined and wept and shouted by turns, reproaching, threatening.

At last she sat back with an air of resolve and blew her nose. "It's no use, Charles." She spoke with finality. "You'll have to give up the group and stay home nights. It's time you became a proper husband and father. I expect it—for me and the children."

She expected it. Suddenly he heard his father's voice, saw his mother's mournful face, felt once more the metal edges of the photo frame slipped into his hand. All his life he'd been asked to meet other people's expectations. What about *his* expectations? *His* life?

Had she guessed what he was thinking? Or had he spoken aloud? For now she said, as though in response, "Your life is here." She moved her hand, her arm, in a gesture encompassing the room, the house, herself. Her face changed. She stood up and moved toward him with a look of entreaty. He took a step back, away from her, but she wrapped her arms around him and fitted her body close to his. "I love you, Charles," she murmured. "I do." While she kissed him, she moved a hand downward, murmuring, caressing.

They went to bed. But he seemed to stand outside the scene like a third party, a neutral observer looking down at the man and woman who lay there. She was using her body as she'd used the children, he thought, to keep him obedient, quiescent. He saw that she was absolutely determined to have her own way. She would never be satisfied with anything less than total surrender.

· · ·

The rocking had stopped. He waited, but there was no further sound. One twenty-five. He had to get up to use the toilet. Might as well take a pill, too, while he was at it.

He got out of bed and tiptoed to the bathroom. Returning, he paused outside the door of the room that had once been Fay's and his. Silence. But light came from under the door. So far he had deliberately kept away from this room, had avoided even glancing through the open doorway whenever he passed. But now he quietly opened the door and entered.

Light from the bedside lamp revealed Ella lying asleep on the bed, on top of the covers. She was still fully dressed except for her shoes.

He went closer. This wasn't the heavy mahogany double bed he remembered; this one was twin-sized, with a maple headboard. That rocking chair? Yes, it was the one Fay had bought all those years before, when she was pregnant with Lois. She had found it at an auction and borne it triumphantly home. He went over to the bureau—cherry, with a bowed front, he didn't recall it—and inspected the photographs that stood on top. One showed a boy of about sixteen, dark-haired, thin-faced, smiling with a hint of uncertainty, perched on some rocks against a glimpse of ocean. The other showed a girl who seemed about twelve, seated on horseback. She had straight blond hair with bangs, and her smile revealed braces.

On the wall nearby hung a frame containing some lines of print. "Never to have heard the soul's puny whisper . . ." A poem. Diane's name was at the bottom. He read it through, trying to make sense of it, then read it through again. Published. Who would have published it?

He went over to the bed and stood looking at Ella. If he had known, would he have returned? Easy enough after all these years to supply an answer. But—the truth? The truth was, he would not have come back. Not then. He'd felt he'd escaped from that house, that life, just in time, flinging out in fury and something like panic after a terrible scene that had gone on for hours. Not even the thought of his two children, nor even an Ella—or perhaps, since the time had come for truth, especially not an Ella—could have brought him back then. There were occasions, after he'd first left, when thoughts of the children had haunted him. Passing a school playground, he'd glimpsed a little girl playing hopscotch who reminded him, in her earnestness, of Lois; he had stood watching till he realized that adults in the playground, probably teachers, were keeping a wary eye on him. Another time, playing a concert in a park on a summer's evening, he'd seen a man in the audience holding a small child on his lap who was gleefully rocking back and forth to the music. At such moments, memory stabbed. Several times, as Fay's due date approached, he had felt a qualm and some curiosity, although the reality of this third child—the child Fay had planned in order to keep him in line—never quite came into focus. But despite all this, he wouldn't have gone back. His new life was precarious and lonely, but at least he could be what he wanted, play what he wanted, come and go as he wished. Going back would have been like going back to jail, with Fay as the warden.

One thing, though; they could say what they liked, think what they liked, but he had tried to keep in touch. Not with Fay but with the children. They had been too young to know that, of course, but he had written, he had telephoned. And he had sent money whenever he could, though it hadn't been easy—he'd left with only his clothes, a few hundred dollars, and their five-year-old car. He'd had no plan, no job, no clear idea of what he would do in the future. His only thought had been to escape from this woman who turned his life into misery and allowed no choices but her own. But he certainly hadn't planned to break with the children. As time passed and they grew older, they would come to visit him, he'd reasoned. And perhaps he would go east to see them. He'd be able to explain everything to them then; he would try to make them understand. Meanwhile, he would do all he could to stay in touch.

But Fay, of course, had intercepted his letters. Whenever he'd telephoned, she'd refused, with a jeering laugh, to put the children on the line. "Come home if you want to talk to them!"

"What kind of blackmail—"

"What kind of man walks out on his children and his pregnant wife?"

"Fay, we can't live together. We're not good for each other. Let's discuss—"

"Come back! Otherwise there's nothing to discuss."

"Fay—"

"If you don't come back, you'll never see the children again! I mean it!" She hung up.

When he next tried to call, he found she had gotten an unlisted number.

After a couple of years he stopped writing. After a while he stopped sending money, too. If she was going to rob him of his children, she could damn well take care of them herself. She could always teach. The house was halfway paid for. She'd inherited some money from Lydia, and there'd be more when Phoebe died. He himself was living from hand to mouth just then.

As time passed the mental pictures he had of Fay and the children began to fade. With each year they lost a little more substance. Gradually all the facets of his former life—Fay's voice, warm and grating by turns; her touch as their bodies moved together; Lois's sober demeanor; Diane's light blue eyes, which matched his own; the house with its plain, high-ceilinged rooms; the faces of certain students and colleagues at the Adler School— began to seem like snippets from an old movie or passages from a book read in early youth.

When notice of the divorce reached him years later, it seemed to make very little difference. By then all the ties had weakened and disintegrated. He was free.

●   ●   ●

Ella stirred, muttering. Her hand went up and scratched her neck, then she was still.

The moments slipped away while he stood watching. Finally he took the afghan from the foot of the bed and covered her with it, then turned off the lamp and left the room.

CHAPTER 6 . . .

"We do what we can, as soon as we can, as well as we can," said the framed legend that hung on the wall.

Lois checked her watch. She had been waiting for more than an hour here in the outer office. What on earth were they doing? Was Ella having—or giving—difficulty?

Please, let this work out. Let something go right, for once.

As Diane had predicted, Ella had refused to leave the house without Charles. Even after Lois had conceded, it was still touch and go. Charles had to remind Ella they would visit Brookfield afterward. He had to allow her to open the car roof, though the day was chilly, and Lois, seated in the back, was thoroughly blown about as they drove. When they arrived, Ella clung to Charles so fiercely that Mrs. Corry let him go along to the testing and interview. Which was fine with Lois; she certainly wasn't eager to be alone with Charles. In the house she kept as far away from him as possible.

Still, she saw now what Diane had meant: Charles seemed able to handle Ella in a way that not even Fay had always managed. Whenever Fay had tried to interest Ella in playing the piano, for example, Ella only pounded the keys angrily with the flat of her hands. Once she had knocked the piano lid down on Fay's hands. Fortunately Fay hadn't been badly hurt, and it was never really clear whether Ella had done it on purpose or accidentally, but Fay had given up after that. Yet last night Ella had rejected her usual television shows for a piano lesson from Charles. She had watched him play an easy scale, then slowly, painstakingly repeated it after him, fingers creeping doggedly from note to note, hitting wrong ones half the time, ascending, then descending. "That's it, you're getting there. Now again." Over and over she tried, clumsy but determined. Afterward she begged, "Play! Play!" and he filled the room with an upbeat tempo, singing along lightly in a style that owed more to phrasing than to quality of voice. "Grab your coat and get your hat, Leave your worry on the doorstep, Just direct your feet, To the sunny side of the street. . . ."

"Sunny-sunny," Ella joined in, raspingly. Chortling, she jiggled her shoulders in time to the music.

The sight of Ella taking instruction not only willingly but eagerly, and trying hard to do her best, startled and moved Lois. At the same time the sight of this man seated at her mother's piano, playing that music, brought a passionate resentment on her mother's behalf. Fay had always detested any form of jazz—vocals, instrumentals, swing, boogie, ragtime. Whenever she heard it played on radio or television—by big bands, small groups, soloists, with or without vocals—she always switched it off.

Once, when Lois was in high school, a boy she knew had brought over some records belonging to his older brother who played saxophone in his college stage band. He put on a record, turned on the record player.

The first notes had barely sounded before Fay whirled into the room. "Turn that off!"

The boy gaped. "It's Paul Desmond—"

"I don't care who it is! If you want to listen to trash, do it somewhere else!"

"Mother!" Lois felt humiliated, close to tears. Not because of the music, she didn't care about the music, but she cared about the boy, who now retreated in disarray. "You spoil everything!" she cried.

"Not me." Fay shook her head. "Put the blame where it belongs."

Years later, when Ella developed a fondness for rock, Fay didn't object. By then Lois understood: regardless of what her mother thought of that music, it didn't evoke the same unhappy memories.

And now the source of those memories sat here, playing the piano. It was disgraceful. She must put a stop to it. But look how Ella was enjoying it, laughing, clapping her hands. Why deprive Ella? Oh, it was too much! She hurried from the room and went upstairs, escaping from the sight and sound. There were things in the attic that needed packing; she would get on with that.

An hour later she came down to find them watching television.

"It's nearly ten o'clock, Ella. You ought to go to bed. We have to be up early tomorrow."

For reply, Ella burst into screeching laughter at something on the screen. With a mental shrug, Lois left them. The program would soon be over.

From the kitchen she heard the program end; minutes later she heard Ella go upstairs. She waited for the sound of rocking. It didn't come. Nor was there any further sound from the living room. He must have gone up, too. But when she went in to turn off the lights, there he was, reading.

"Oh. I thought you'd gone to bed."

"Do you mind if I stay down here for a while?"

"Suit yourself. Turn off the lights when you're through." She started for the stairs.

"Lois—" She halted, not turning. "Is there some way we can talk, you and I?"

"I've nothing to say to you."

"Would you listen then?"

"I'm really not interested in anything you have to tell me."

The telephone rang. She hurried back to the kitchen to answer. It might be Gordon. He hadn't been home when she left this afternoon. They had been polite but distant with each other since that last exchange, keeping out of each other's way like strangers—or worse, enemies. Perhaps he was calling now to put things right. Perhaps he had seen the truth of her words and—

But it wasn't Gordon; it was just some man asking for Diane. Rather an attractive voice. She said Diane was away, wouldn't be back for a while. He said he was calling from New York, had just returned from abroad. Was there a number where he might reach her?

"She's in Cleveland. Just a minute."

She gave him the number of the hotel where Diane was staying. He thanked her and hung up.

She went upstairs and got ready for bed. Lucky Diane, flown off to Cleveland, away from problems. Oh, to be flying away somewhere, anywhere, the farther the better. No need, while aloft, to find answers, take action; until you touched down, you were free from the troubles that awaited below. The airlines were missing a sure thing—there must be thousands of people who would pay a good price to stay endlessly airborne. *We take our time getting you there*, the airlines would promise.

You could achieve the same effect, of course, with liquor or drugs. Not quite the same. Being drunk or drugged took your mind from your troubles but didn't remove you physically; you were still there, right on the spot, caught in situations requiring you to start, stop, decide, take steps. She herself wasn't much inclined, anyway, to alcohol or pills; liquor in quantity only made her sick, and she was too prudent to allow herself even an aspirin unless it was strictly necessary. Prudence, moderation. Those were her watchwords.

Too much so?

She stopped brushing her teeth and stared at herself in the

mirror. Never once had she gotten drunk; never once had she slept with anyone besides Gordon. Even with Gordon, she had never really gone as far as she suspected one could go. Even when they were first married, their lovemaking had never been more than— well, functional. Perhaps she simply wasn't a very physical person. Or perhaps Gordon—? She might have followed his lead if he'd been more venturesome, but he didn't seem constituted that way. Still, this hadn't ever seriously troubled her, so long as everything else had been all right.

She got into bed and made a stringent effort to direct her thoughts to subjects that wouldn't keep sleep at bay. She had to finish that report on fund-raising for the new day-care center on campus. They were almost out of kaolin at the Shed. She must remember to call the dentist; Amy needed an appointment for when she next came home. At Thanksgiving. Six weeks away.

Thanksgiving.

The previous year, as Christmas approached, Lois had begun to nurse a hope that the holiday season might bring Ned home. At such a time he surely couldn't help thinking about family, and the familiar setting, known rituals, material comforts of home. Even if he came home only overnight, and gave some indication that he was getting tired of the way he was living, he might, with the holiday approaching, be more open to persuasion.

But Christmas and New Year's, with all their emotional weight, had come and gone without a word. Not even a card. So now she tried to tell herself not to hope. But she couldn't stop her thoughts. She couldn't obliterate the pictures, which rose like uninvited ghosts . . . Ned sleeping in a doorway, behind the un-availing shelter of a cardboard box . . . Ned huddled under a bridge . . . Ned lying on a park bench, newspapers flapping . . .

She sat up abruptly and switched on the lamp. It might help to read for a while.

Then she heard the sound of the rocking chair. Almost, she welcomed it as she got out of bed and went to Fay's room.

Ella, dressed in her long printed nightgown, was rocking steadily, but something was different: the movement was slower, less frantic. She seemed relaxed, almost to the point of drowsiness. Her eyes were closed and she hummed tunelessly as she rocked back and forth.

Lois sat down on the bed. So far they had changed very little in here. Fay's clothes were still in the closet. The framed photographs were still on the bureau, including one of Ned at the Cape on their last family vacation. He and Karen had just started going together then; they hadn't yet reached the stage where Ned wouldn't go anywhere without her. And here was the picture of Amy that Fay had always liked—Amy seated on Royal, smiling broadly, one hand raised in a wave. Over there on the wall was Diane's poem, framed, from the days when she'd worked for that magazine, *Slings, Wings*, something like that. Fay had kept it all this time. For a parent, the efforts of a son or daughter at any age always retained value, of course. Still, as a gift to be cherished, how could even the finest poem, let alone that pretentious claptrap, begin to compare with those two young faces smiling in the photographs? And now, *now*, which of Fay's daughters had rejected the man who had ruined Fay's life? Which one had allowed him to stay, let him back into their lives? So it was, and had always been, yet she had never caught up with Diane in Fay's estimation. Bitterness tasted like rust in her mouth.

She stood. "Come on, Ella. Bedtime."

Ella opened her eyes. Still humming, she left the rocker and climbed into bed.

Lois started to turn off the lamp, then noticed something on the pillow. "What's that?"

Ella showed her. It was a nightgown rolled into a small bundle. "Mama's." She lay down, tucking it under her face, and rubbed her cheek back and forth against it.

Lois laid a hand on Ella's hair. "Sleep tight, Lella." It was the name Ned, as a child, had given her.

Back in her room, she felt more than ready for sleep as she turned out the light and lay down. But a muddled slide show rose in the dark, out of sequence . . . Ned, aged two, trailing his blanket around the house, tucking it under his face when he slept . . . Fay at the piano, late at night, the silvery sound of "Clair de Lune," moonlight shining on deep, dark water . . . In a room smelling of disinfectant, an old, old woman, Aunt Phoebe, whipped out her teeth and grinned at their looks of horror. Only Ella, three years old, found it funny and laughed.

Then came something she hadn't thought of for years. Was she six, seven, that time she'd overheard Fay talking on the telephone, voice shrill with malevolence . . . "Can't I, though? Wait! You'll find out!" Fear had racked her as she heard that vengeful tone, though the words themselves had held no meaning. Fay had slammed down the receiver, then caught sight of Lois. She had knelt and put her arms around her. "He'll find out!" she whispered.

•   •   •

The door from the inner office opened. Mrs. Corry beckoned.

The news was good. The center would accept Ella as a client in its Work Experience program. She would work at a place called The Country Store, a retail outlet for baked goods and other foods made on the premises by people in the program. If she wished, she could start the following Monday. Meanwhile, she should visit the store—not today, but the next day or later in the week. A visit would help allay any fears, would help set at rest inevitable nervousness.

Lois felt light-headed with relief, almost jubilant, as she listened. There was only one hitch at the moment, Mrs. Corry said. "Our clients live in group homes. They walk to work or come by bus. But there isn't a home vacancy at present."

That didn't matter right now, Lois told her. At present Ella was living at home. After that she could stay with Lois until a vacancy opened up.

Ella would work a six-hour day. She'd be paid an hourly rate based on minimum wages. She would also receive counseling and basic instruction in reading and writing, survival skills. . . .

The more Lois heard, the better it sounded. But as she filled in forms and signed papers, caution reasserted itself. Would Ella be willing to visit The Country Store? And would she then agree to start work?

From the center they went to Brookfield Gardens, as Charles had promised. The outing was not a success. At the greenhouse, one of the gardeners scolded Ella when she kept reaching out to touch the flowering plants. When a little boy did the same thing, Ella shouted, "No touching!" so loudly that the child burst into tears, and Ella backed away, looking scared.

At home later she grew rambunctious. No, she didn't *want* to watch a show, she didn't *want* to play the piano, she didn't *want* to help get dinner ready. She snatched up a plate, held it high, looked at Lois defiantly, then let it drop. Then she rushed upstairs, and seconds later the sound of rocking began, fast, frenetic.

Charles swept up the shattered fragments. "It's been a hard day for her."

"You needn't explain. *I've* lived with her," Lois said pointedly. She stood at the counter, preparing dinner.

"Can I help?"

"You could peel those carrots and onions."

The blare of rock music was suddenly added to the thump of the rocking chair.

Charles looked dismayed. "She likes that?"

"Yes. That's her radio. She sometimes holds it while she rocks."

The music swelled to an earsplitting level. Charles left the kitchen and went upstairs. Minutes later the music dropped to a tolerable volume.

He returned. "Shall I do the potatoes, too?"

She nodded.

He worked efficiently, she noticed. Was he used to cooking for himself?

"Do you cook?" she asked.

"After a fashion. In my time I've done a little of everything."

His time. Did a little of everything include a stint as short-order cook? She started to ask, then stopped. To question was to show interest.

Using the knife, he pushed the cut-up vegetables into a bowl. "I've been meaning to ask—did Ella ever go to school?"

"Until seventh grade. Then Mother took her out. All she'd learned by then was to read simple words and write her name and some numbers. The other kids gave her a hard time. The teachers said she was disruptive."

"Wasn't there a special school—"

"Yes. But it was really for people who were much worse off, and Mother felt Ella would only regress there. From then on she kept her at home and taught her as much as she could herself." She ran water into a saucepan and put it on the stove. "I guess I have to thank you for your help today. Ella wouldn't have gone without you."

"She ought to go and see the store tomorrow. I don't think too much time should elapse."

"I agree. But will she go, do you think?"

He shrugged. "We'll see."

We.

All right. His help was definitely needed for this. Next week, too. So be it. In this small way, let him begin to redress the balance. Let him repay the smallest fraction of what he owed.

When Ella was called for dinner, she refused to come down. Charles went up to talk to her and returned to report that she wanted dinner upstairs.

Lois shook her head. "She has to come down if she's hungry."

"So I told her." He set the table while Lois dished out. They sat down to eat.

"Are those your children in the photos upstairs? Tell me about them."

"Why?"

"Why?" He looked taken aback. "I'm interested. They're my grandchildren."

You have to earn grandchildren, she almost said, but decided not to. "Amy's fifteen. Ned"—merely saying his name hurt— "Ned's nineteen."

"Away at school?"

"Not right now." She took a sip of water. "Amy's at school, in Connecticut . . ." Her tone warmed as she went on talking about Amy.

Suddenly Ella appeared in the doorway. She had taken off her shoes and stockings. Her long, bare feet gleamed white against the dark floor.

"Hello, there," Charles said.

She padded over. Standing by the table, she reached out a hand. Lois tensed. Ella picked up a fork, speared a piece of meat from Charles's plate, and put it in her mouth. Then, with a bump, she sat down. "Hungry."

● ● ●

When dinner was over, Ella and Charles went to the piano. Lois went upstairs to look for a blouse of Ella's that she knew needed repair. She found it and stayed up there, sitting on the bed while she sewed. The sound of Ella working on a scale filtered up from below. "Do, re, mi, fa, sol, la . . ." Slowly, with many mistakes, but trying over and over. Fay would have been hurt to see Charles succeed where she had failed. Still, this was surely good for Ella. Whatever his motive, whatever his reasons, he was good for Ella in all sorts of ways. Should loyalty to Fay interfere with that?

"Now you!" she heard Ella command. "Play!"

Charles swung into a tune. Something familiar, yet she couldn't quite place it. And then she did. "Red sails in the sunset, 'way out on the sea . . ." But he wasn't playing it slowly, as it was usually done, but quite fast, so that it was cheerful, jaunty. You could almost picture someone tap-dancing.

"No!" Ella cried. "Sunny-sunny! Sunny-sunny!"

The music stopped abruptly as the doorbell sounded. She heard Charles go to the door. Seconds later he called her.

She hurried downstairs.

"Oh—Mario—" What on earth could he want? "How are you?" she asked politely.

"Okay, I guess." He sounded as pleased to see her as she was to see him. "Here." He held out a bottle, gift-wrapped.

"How nice. Thank you." She tried to appear suitably grateful. "That's very welcome."

Charles had slipped away, thank heaven. The mere thought of introducing these two—Mario, this is Mother's ex; Charles, this is Mother's lover—was mind-boggling.

Ella appeared. She stared balefully.

"Hi, Ella," Mario said. "How's it going?"

Glowering, Ella trudged past him and up the stairs.

He shook his head ruefully. "Great to be popular."

"Oh, you know Ella."

He shifted his weight from one foot to the other. "Is Diane around?"

"Diane's away."

"Away?" He looked surprised. "I guess you weren't expecting me then." He explained that Diane had invited him over.

Oh, dear. Just like Diane, to invite someone and then forget all about it.

"She had to leave town suddenly, on business."

"Guess I'll be getting along then. Sorry I bothered you." He turned to go.

At this she felt conscience-stricken. It wasn't his fault, after all. "Won't you stay and have a drink? We'll put this to use." She held up the bottle.

For a second he hesitated. Then, "Thanks," he said. "Sounds like a good idea."

He followed her into the pantry, where she poured the drinks. He no longer helped himself, she noticed. Of course, with Fay gone, he was no longer the man of the house, so to speak. She studied him surreptitiously as they sat in the kitchen. Creamy shirt spread open at the neck. Silver pendant. But there was something different. He carried himself more formally, like a guest. He seemed more serious, too, even somber. Well, naturally. But perhaps that was why he seemed different from the way she remembered. Or was it just that she saw him in a different light now that Fay was gone?

The ceiling trembled as Ella began to rock.

He looked startled. "What's that?"

"Ella. She's taken to rocking in Mother's chair ever since she died."

His face changed. "Poor kid . . ."

His gaze moved around slowly, rested for a moment on the well-used stove, traveled to the bins, moved to the notepad fixed beside the telephone, where Fay had jotted down orders.

He raised his glass. "To Fay."

The liquor slid smoothly down her throat.

He told her Diane had mentioned a photograph of Fay taken some time back, for business. She had said she would look out a spare print for him. Did Lois by any chance know the one Diane meant?

Lois pondered. "I think so."

She went away and came back with the photograph a few minutes later.

Together they studied it, an eight-by-ten print showing a slightly younger Fay in her butcher apron, laughing as she stirred something in a bowl.

"Was this taken here?"

"Yes. For a flyer about cooking classes."

"She taught classes here? In the house?"

"Yes. But she stopped them after a few sessions."

"Why?"

"Well, Ella interfered. She did no harm, but some people were bothered. Mother tried to get her to stay in her room while the class was going on, but—" She shrugged.

Mario gazed at the photo. "She looks so alive, enthusiastic. She always threw herself completely into whatever she was doing."

True, Lois thought. Fay had never done anything by halves. Including loving. Or hating.

He slid the picture back in the envelope. "Are you sure you can spare this?"

"Yes, we have others."

The sound of rocking stopped. The sudden quiet was faintly unnerving. Into the silence came other sounds: Charles moving about his room.

She saw Mario glance upward. Was he wondering? Let him wonder. She wasn't obliged to explain.

"When are you planning to move?"

"We have to be out by December tenth."

"What about Ella?"

"Her name's down for a group home. If all goes well, she may have a job."

His eyes widened. "What kind of job?"

Lois told him.

"Sounds right up her alley," he said. "I hope it works out." He went to the pantry and brought back the bottle. Without asking, he refilled her glass and then his own. He swirled the liquor around in his glass. "Fay was always worried about Ella. You knew that, I guess."

Oh, yes, she knew. She had always tried to encourage Fay to work less and go out more and increase her circle of friends, but it was always difficult to get her to leave Ella. The most she would do was go out for an occasional evening, if she could find someone to stay with Ella. But even then Ella made things hard. For Fay's fiftieth birthday, Lois and Gordon had given her a Caribbean cruise. Lois offered to have Ella stay with them while Fay was gone, but Fay said that wouldn't work. "You know Ella's unhappy out of the house unless I'm with her." "For once she'll do as she's told," Lois said. "You can't be Ella's prisoner for the rest of your life."

But when Ella, as predicted, wept and refused to cooperate, and it seemed Fay really might not go, Lois moved over to Fay's for the time she was gone.

As Lois hoped, Fay did meet someone on the cruise—Dudley Cross, an anesthesiologist from Pittsburgh, widowed and retired, though hardly retiring: he talked nonstop. He came to Shelburne a couple of times after that to see Fay, and Fay went to Pittsburgh once, for a weekend. But that was as far as it went. "Not my type," was all Fay said when Lois asked her why.

Fay had also gone out briefly with Herb Porter, who handled the legal work in connection with her business. But soon that stopped, too.

Gordon said the real reason was Ella. He said it always grew clear to anyone interested in Fay that, one way or another, Ella had to be part of the package. Perhaps he was right. On the other hand, perhaps Fay simply wasn't receptive.

"Why would she be, to either of those two?" Diane asked when Lois mentioned it. "Dudley never shuts up for a second; he must have talked his patients to sleep without benefit of ether. And Herb's all right, but dull as dishwater."

"That may be *your* opinion—"

"Mother's, too. She told me."

So Fay had talked to Diane about it, but not to her. Perhaps because she knew Lois wouldn't agree with her estimate. Of course, Fay was always hard on men. It was easy to understand why, but the fact remained.

.   .   .

"Yes," Lois said. "Mother's whole life was ruled by Ella."

"Ruined?"

"Ruled. Well—ruined, too."

Mario leaned back. "I'm not so sure. Of course, from my point of view, it wasn't a good situation. You knew I wanted to marry Fay?"

"Yes. But Ella put you off." It was more statement than question.

His answer surprised her.

"No, that wasn't it. I was prepared to live with Ella. But because of Ella, Fay wouldn't have me. She knew Ella didn't like me. Ella was jealous of anyone who took Fay's attention. Still, I think we could have worked it out if Fay had been willing to try."

"She gave up everything, over and over, for Ella." What a waste. What a pity.

"That's what I thought, at first. That she was sacrificing herself to Ella." He leaned forward. "That wasn't it, though. She wanted it that way—Ella with her all the time, dependent on her."

"Wanted? Why would she? Why would anyone—?"

"Beats me. I argued it with her often enough. Well . . ." He finished his drink. "Water under the bridge now . . ."

The clock chimed in the hall. Mario stood up. "Give Diane my best. And good luck with Ella. If I can help with moving, anything, call me. Don't forget."

She thanked him and went with him to the door. The pendant gleamed against his skin, descending into the V of his shirt. She held out her hand. "I'm glad you came over. I wish . . ." She hesitated. "Perhaps we could talk some more sometime. About Mother. I'd like . . ." Her voice trailed off. I'd like to know how it was between you. Why it worked so well for you and her, but not for her and the man she married.

"I'd like that, too."

The hand holding hers was warm and firm. She stared at the

shadows where the pendant nestled. For an instant she wanted to reach out and touch that V.

Mario said softly, "Right now, you look just like her." Suddenly he leaned forward and kissed her.

She smelled a musky odor, mingled with—aftershave, was it? Or something on his hair? Then he was gone. She stood, startled, not only at the kiss but at her body's secret response. Face hot, blood surging, she watched him drive away.

CHAPTER 7 . . .

At the hotel the elevator door slid open, revealing passengers clad in corporate sobriety, charcoal, navy, brown. Briefcase in hand, Diane stepped inside, adding taupe to the spectrum. Tailored suit, white blouse, small gold earrings. Lois would approve. Here I am in Cleveland, in my other persona. Glad to be in Cleveland, away from Lois and—yes, forgive, please—from Ella, too. And from the house that, since Fay's death, held sadness as a draped piece of cloth holds shadows in its folds. How were Lois and Charlie getting along? However, whatever, she wasn't going to worry. Not now. Just now, thanks to Jake, she was free from all that. Allee-allee-home-freeee.

The elevator dropped like a plumb down fifteen stories, then disgorged its occupants. As she crossed the lobby, she glimpsed someone who looked like Adam walking ahead. Then he turned to speak to a companion, and she saw that though he was broad-shouldered and stocky like Adam, with the same decisive stride, he really didn't look at all like him.

Ever since Adam had left, she'd been seeing him everywhere: getting out of a cab, going into a restaurant, buying tickets for a movie. In Shelburne, too, she sometimes glimpsed him crossing the street, checking out at the supermarket, backing a car out of a driveway. Early one evening a neighbor had come to the door to inquire about a lost dog, and just for a second, in the half dusk, her heart had shifted gears.

Probably, she told herself as she hailed a cab, he didn't even look exactly as she remembered. After three months in the Solomon Islands he'd be very tan, for one thing. A little heavier, perhaps. Or thinner. With a different haircut. No haircut. A beard. The voice, though, would be the same, those deep, warm tones an interesting contrast with the face with the broken nose, souvenir of a fall from a tree in early childhood. He looked like a thoughtful pugilist. How had he avoided a career on the airwaves? she'd asked. He'd fall back on that, he said, if geology failed. Seismology, to be precise, the science and study of earthquakes, their causes, effects, and attendant phenomena . . . great cataclysmic rendings and explosions, upheavals great and small, faint subterranean tremors manifested by the slow bending and unbending of the earth's surface, deep shudders indicating more to follow.

Out of the cab, across the street, and into another elevator, which snapped shut around a dozen victims. In cathedral silence, up they rocketed. A miracle! How was it they only stood reading the headlines or watching the indicator light for their floor? Once, vacationing in the south of France, she had taken a local bus from Nice to the village of Èze, perched high in the rocky landscape. It was late October, and only a few of the passengers were tourists; the others were people who lived there and made the trip frequently. She had never seen such glorious vistas as she saw from the windows of that bus: Nice, the harbor, the Baie des Anges, then Beaulieu, Cap Ferrat, Villefranche, Cap d'Antibes jutting into the sea . . . Yet the man sitting in front of her never so much as glanced out, gave all his attention to his newspaper. Two women sitting farther along the bus were totally absorbed in a discussion of the best way to cook a *pistou*. A pair of small boys kept their heads bent over some kind of dice game. Most of the others either chatted or seemed lost in thought. Of course, if you did this every day . . .

This business of *every day*. Where you lived, whom you lived with, what you worked at, played at. She'd waited for it to happen with Adam, but it hadn't so far. Of course, though she'd known him now for over a year, they had actually lived together for only two months before he'd left for the Solomons. At that point everything had still been as good between them as when he'd moved in. All of it. They even liked each other's friends.

Every relationship she'd ever had before this one had begun to curve gradually but ineluctably downward as the weeks went by. As soon as she felt that start to happen, she always withdrew. Why wait around for things to become difficult or tedious? Not that she never had regrets, brief moments of wondering whether she'd done the right thing. Especially over Michel. Her friend Gretchen had declared herself baffled, over Michel especially.

"Of course, I see the problem," Gretchen had said. "Why would you want a man who's smart, sexy, and crazy about you? You're even both in the same line of work."

"Hardly."

"You both write, anyway. And living in Paris wouldn't be hard to take. Listen"—she erased a line from the sketch she was making of a sweater—"you can't go on like this forever."

"I don't notice *you* settling down."

"Settling?" She stared at the sketch with narrowed eyes. "Husband and kids? Not yet. But I'd go for something steady, yes, if I could find a good man, not neurotic or immature or—"

"Come on, Gretchen, there are men around."

"*You* seem to find them, I notice, though you drop them ten minutes later. How you could pass up Michel—!" She shook her pencil in warning. "It won't always be so easy. For one thing, we're not twenty-one anymore."

Diane smiled. "You mean, Michel could have been my old-age insurance? My . . . ace in the hole, as it were?"

Gretchen sighed. "Don't you ever take anything seriously?"

"Yes. But not forever." *Forever* was a term she disliked. The word seemed to glow red, like a road sign warning DETOUR or SLOW. *Tu es lâche*, Michel had accused. Coward? No, he didn't understand. To be fair, how could he when she herself didn't?

"Have you thought of seeing an analyst?" Gretchen asked.

"Not seriously."

Gretchen flung an eraser at her.

●　　　●　　　●

The man sitting behind the desk swiveled around so that he faced the window, then seconds later swiveled back to face her. If he kept on like this, she was going to get motion-sick. A kind of nervous tic, this swiveling. What was the line from that Danny Kaye movie—Adam would know the title instantly—" 'Can you dance?' 'Yes, I taught St. Vitus.' "

"You saw the piece that was done about six years ago? The information's right, but the tone ought to be less—less—"

"Incantatory?"

"Exactly."

She wrote steadily as they went on talking, her reflections a steady counterpoint to their voices. These days Kandex manufactured a broad range of products, but it had gotten its start with, of all things, the zipper. Imagine, this forty-story tower, the factories here and abroad, those figures in the annual report, all from the humble zipper. Which still accounted for considerable profits. There were zippers on everything nowadays.

Ideas bloomed as they talked. Her pen hurried to keep up. Thank God for the safety net of the tape recorder. To start: turn-of-the-century woman struggling to do up dozens of tiny buttons running from neck to waist of dress. Good. For graphics, too. A man buttoning boots? His fly? (Stop that, no time for levity.

When did they first put zippers on pants? Did Brooks still make them with buttons? Ask Adam.)

•   •   •

"Madam, I'm Adam," he'd said, by way of introduction. "That's a palindrome. Oldest in existence."

"I thought the oldest was in the Museum of Natural History," she'd said demurely.

"Ah!" Smiling, he raised his voice to be heard above the hubbub. Would she care to leave this party and go with him to see the palindrome?

She would. She did.

At the museum he led her past the fossil collections—"Only anagrams in there"—and, standing in front of a vast dinosaur skeleton, delivered a brief lecture on the species *Palindromus maximus*, not quite extinct.

•   •   •

"There's a lot of useful stuff in the history of the first plant, the one in Columbus."

"Is it true Walter Meldrum used to work on the line?" she asked.

"Yes. There are wonderful stories about Walter. Be sure to talk to Harry Beebe, he'll tell you all kinds of tales about those early days. . . ."

Strange, she was invariably nervous at the start of a project, but always, no matter how dull the subject first appeared, possibilities slowly began to come clear, like a photographic image coming up in the chemical bath. Specifics began to take form: a good lead, done in scene, visual, an angle, tone, quotes to add life, anecdotes for interest and color, a strong conclusion—all the things that made her, she knew, very good at this.

When she looked back now on the poems! How could she ever have imagined—? At least she had finally acknowledged the truth and put it behind her. It was surely better to do this kind of thing well than to write bad poetry. She found considerable satisfaction in rising to the challenge and bringing it off each time. Being not only paid but praised for a job well done. And the money was good.

"Be sure to include . . ." He checked off points one by one on his fingers.

Swiveling notwithstanding, this man, who looked like a keen-eyed greyhound, knew what he wanted. Not a ditherer. You didn't get to this rung of the ladder by dithering. His office was tastefully decorated with Oriental art—scrolls, screens, porcelain. Had he chosen these pieces himself? He'd given a sharp look of appraisal when she'd walked in today, and a cordial but businesslike hand-shake, recalling their previous meeting. She felt a certain respect for his clear thinking, his unfussy authority.

Most of the time she felt alien to the people she dealt with, who seemed interchangeable in their uniforms of correct suit, tie, weight, tan, political beliefs. "Troublemakers," said the vice-president of a utility for which she had done some work. "March-ing around, 'No nuclear waste on our doorstep.' Don't they realize there are things you have to accept if you want a decent standard of living?" She kept quiet always, and wrote. So much for integrity. Lately she'd been thinking she didn't want to do this for the rest of her life, though she didn't yet know what else she might do.

One thing she'd noticed: no matter what level these people reached, they nearly all ran scared. And no wonder. She was offered jobs from time to time as an in-house writer; the salary was good, the benefits were excellent. But she preferred to stay free-lance. Otherwise there'd be no way not to be touched by that fear—fear that kept you on the job even if you hated it; fear of losing those golden benefits; fear of consignment to the scrap heap at forty, forty-five, if you hadn't by then reached a certain level. And along the way, the plotting, politics, any real friendship at work precluded by get-ahead caution.

On a job she'd done in Atlanta, the woman in communications who'd briefed her—a very savvy person—had told her some stories over coffee. "I used to have lunch once or twice a week in the cafeteria here with a woman I was friendly with in the marketing department. One day I came back to find a note on my desk. My boss wanted to see me. Turned out he'd been watching. 'You and Marcy seem to have a lot to talk about,' he said. 'Do you talk business?' I didn't understand at first. 'Sometimes,' I said. 'Mostly, it's personal.' 'Oh, girl talk,' he said. 'Okay. Be careful, though. It's not a good idea to have buddies at the office.' "

Was it any wonder men in business didn't dare let down and talk to each other openly, honestly? Didn't even know how to talk to each other, except on the most superficial level?

Adam was as different from that as night from day. Untouched by fear—that kind of fear, anyway. He had a quiet sureness about himself and his abilities that she found only rarely in the men she worked with. And . . . he made her laugh. She liked that. She made him laugh, too. When she shouldn't, sometimes.

"Look at that." He glanced down at himself. "Look what you've done."

"I'm sorry," she said, penitent. "Let's start over. I'll shut up."

He sighed. "I don't want you to shut up. I just want you to be serious when the occasion requires it."

In bed, before, was one of those occasions. She knew that. Jokes were death to lovemaking, no erection could survive them. So why did she do it?

She'd been more careful after that whenever they made love. But there were still other times when, at the mere approach of certain subjects, she turned flippant.

"Why do you do that?" he demanded. "Why won't you talk? What are you afraid of?"

"Afraid?" In her head a bell rang. *Lâche.*

"I've been trying for some time now to discuss our future—"

"Stop!"

"Stop what?"

"Sounding . . . pompous." That was unfair. She knew it the minute she said it.

He seized her firmly. "This is the umpteenth time I've tried to say this, but each time you've deflected me. I'll be brief: I love and admire you, I'd like to marry you. What do you say?" He gave her a slight shake. "No jokes now. Don't run away. Answer."

She hesitated.

"All right, let's try it the other way around. How do you feel about me? Do you love me? Are you willing to consider my proposal? Jesus, I sound like Jane Austen."

"Can't we just go on as we are? It's lovely like this."

"Diane, listen. I'm forty-two years old. I've been through the average number of wars, domestic and foreign, I pay alimony and child support, my hairline's receding. That's the bad news. There's some good news, too, and you know what it is. Put your good news with mine, we're a hell of a team. Oh, God"—he put his head in his hands—"that's not the way to say it, it's not what I mean."

"Love, I know what you mean." She stroked his hair. True, it was receding.

"Are you listening to me?"

"Yes. I'm mulling."

Lâche. Was it true? Was she afraid? If so, of what? Permanence? Stability, as exemplified by Lois and Gordon? Loss of freedom, autonomy?

"Diane, tell me, what do you want from life?"

She said, slowly, "I don't know. Yet. What do you?"

"I have most of what I want. Eric and Matt. Work I enjoy. Friends. And now a lover, companion, friend. If she'll have me. One thing's missing."

"Which is?"

"The word's been done to death, alas: commitment."

"From me?"

"To as much as from. An exchange, even-steven." He smiled. "Don't look so scared."

"I'm not."

"Listen." He took her hand. "I'm leaving next week. Think about it while I'm gone. When I come back, I'd like an answer."

"You mean, yes or no?"

"Fish or cut bait." He put a hand under her chin, tilted her face. "Let's not waste this. We have a many-splendored thing going here."

"Why not leave it at that, then? There'd only be problems."

Impatiently he said, "Of course there'd be problems!"

"Well, then?"

"Well, then," he said.

• • •

Henry Beebe, vice-president and secretary, threw up his arms as she entered. His face was crimson, he seemed apoplectic. "I don't know what you think you're going to do here!"

She smiled, carefully. "I'd like to get some information for the history."

"I know that! But I don't know why in hell they scheduled you for today—I don't have anything ready for you. You might as well turn right around and get out of here."

Holding on to her smile, she spoke quietly. Could they just chat for a while about the early days? His personal recollections? She understood he'd known Walter Meldrum and could tell some fascinating stories about that era. . . .

Gradually he began to talk.

He stared fixedly at her legs as he rambled on. He sent for coffee for them both. By the time she left, he was amiable and positively garrulous, warmed by her appreciation of the unique extent of his personal knowledge. She broke away with difficulty to go to her next appointment.

• • •

"Thought of a title yet?" Frank Vigo asked.

"Not yet. I need all the input first."

"Who's next?"

"Marsden Trotter, Latin America. Then Arthur Dill."

"Trotter's all right, he'll probably tell you more than you really want to know. But Dill . . ." He rolled his eyes. "Art's turned paranoid ever since the merger. Good luck."

●   ●   ●

By the time she was through it was almost six o'clock. Her brain had begun to fuzz, her hand was shaky from taking notes. She would spend the entire evening going over tapes, enlarging her notes while everything was still fresh in her mind. Tomorrow would be more of the same.

Back in her room, she washed up. She was starved. She'd have dinner downstairs in the Garden Room, then come back up to work. Should she call Lois to find out how things had gone with Ella? No, she couldn't face a recital of complaints right now. If there were problems, Lois would call.

Downstairs in the cavernous Garden Room, the decor was Late Funerary. A motif of white wreaths made of lilies was imprinted on the black wallpaper. Stiff arrangements of real lilies bedecked the long buffet table. The waiter who came to take her order looked appropriately cadaverous. A man in chef's garb stood behind the buffet, looking redundant since nearly all the tables were empty. The few diners were widely dispersed, she at one end of the room, a male quartet at the other, their talk punctuated with bursts of laughter that sounded forced. The only other diner was a man sitting alone at a table by a fake window that looked out onto a fake garden. Everything and everyone seemed stultified, ossified—the ambience, the chef, the waiters, the flowers, and the food that was finally placed before her. Perhaps she herself, too, in this setting . . . ?

She always carried something to read when eating out alone. Now she opened her book.

"Excuse me . . ." She looked up to see a man standing there, middle-aged yet baby-faced, a look of anxiety beneath his smile. Where had he sprung from? Then it came to her: this was the man who'd been sitting by the fake window.

"Would you like some company?"

"No, thank you." Formally polite.

"Ah, come on." He lowered his voice. "I mean, I'm alone, you're alone, so—"

"No." She'd found from experience that it paid to be blunt.

"I'm on the road all the time. It gets so you'd like to hear another voice, you know? We'll sit and chat, that's all. Come on. I'll buy you a drink," he said hopefully.

"If you don't go away, I'll call the waiter."

"Okay, take it easy! Christ, anyone would think I wanted to rape you!" He departed, making his way between the empty tables.

Gradually her annoyance subsided. She thought about him. His life beyond the Garden Room. On the road. Years of dinners alone in places like this. Was there a wife back home? Children? Was he divorced? Widowed?

She suddenly regretted that she'd been so curt. She could have done it a little more kindly. She could have said she was waiting for someone or had an appointment. Too late now. He was gone.

For some reason, Charlie came to mind, though he was nothing like this man in appearance or manner.

Then she realized: over the weekend Charlie had told her something about the first years after he'd left. Life on the road, sometimes alone, sometimes with one or two other musicians, looking for gigs, wherever, whatever, a Moose Club dance, a gas station opening, a local fiesta—one-nighters mostly, now and then a week's engagement in a tavern or roadhouse. Occasionally, when he got desperate, he turned to other things. He'd been fruit picker, handyman, door-to-door salesman for an encyclopedia called *The Knowledge of the Universe*. Not eating in places like this, certainly, which, embalmed though it was, wasn't cheap. Nearly everyone who came here was on an expense account.

Listening to him, she had tried to picture him as he must have been then, in his late thirties, vigorous, seized by a passion that had moved him to shuck the role of husband/father/householder. More hair then, and more color. Seeming ordinary, yet set off from ordinary by the music, that gypsy life, those choices. Leery of ties, avoiding all but the most casual encounters. But along the way there must have been women. Singers for the songs he played. And in the bars, the roadhouses, women watching, listening, drawn to him and the music, waiting for him to be through after the final set.

The waiter brought the check. She signed and left. Still lost in thought, she stood waiting for the elevator. When it came, she boarded, pressed the button for her floor, then moved to the back, making room for others. A couple got on, and a man on his own who really looked astonishingly—

Oh! She stared and stared.

He looked at her, smiling.

Very tan, yes. And the sun had bleached his hair.

The elevator door opened. She stood transfixed. He held the door. "Is this your floor?" he asked politely.

Shock, excitement, joy mingled inside her as they walked along the hall.

In her room they held each other. His mouth. Their mouths. "Oh, God, Adam . . ." Her voice was faint. "I have to work tonight."

"Just for a little while . . ."

He might look different, but he sounded just the same, felt just the same.

He unbuttoned her blouse. She unbuttoned his shirt. Brown, everywhere . . .

. . .

Afterward someone went by in the hall, whistling. "Went down to St. James Infirmary, saw my baby there. Stretched out on a long white table, so cold, so pale, so fair. . . ."

Diane stirred reluctantly. "It's getting late, Adam. I have to get to work." With an enormous effort of will, she extricated herself and got out of bed.

"Ah, you women are all alike—one quick one and you're off!" He got up, too, and began to dress, talking all the while. He'd known she'd be busy, so he'd taken a room of his own and brought along some work. "Will you have any free time tomorrow?"

She shook her head. Her first appointment was at seven-thirty, and she'd be tied up every minute after that until she caught the four o'clock flight back to Shelburne.

He made a suggestion: could she stay over one more night? After that they'd go their separate ways. But he'd soon be able to take time off, and then he could spend a few days in Shelburne. "If you like," he added.

"Adam . . ." She paused. If she said yes, come to Shelburne, he might take something for granted that she hadn't yet decided. "I can't really make any definite plans yet about Shelburne. But I will stay over tomorrow." Lois could surely manage for one more day. She'd tell her the job was running longer.

He told her about his project, a study of earthquake zones around the Solomons. The work had gone extremely well; that was why he'd finished and come home sooner than expected.

How were things going in Shelburne? he asked.

She told him about the funeral (he knew about Fay, Diane had called him when she died) and about the plans they were making for Ella and—"Adam, guess what! Guess who dropped by!"

He considered. "An old flame?"

"My father!"

"*What?* You mean your long-lost?"

"The very same."

"Where is he?"

"In Shelburne, at the house. I'm dying to tell you all about it, but—"

"Okay, I'm going." He kissed her, then moved to the door. "I'm in three-seventeen. If you want me"—he made his voice sultry—"just whistle. You know how to whistle, don't you?"

The door opened and closed. He was gone.

●   ●   ●

At one A.M. she was through.

Her travel alarm was set for six. She changed it to six-thirty. If she skipped breakfast, she could still make it.

She picked up the telephone, thinking about whistling, about the earth moving, temblors registering on the Richter scale. Just for a while, then sleep, bodies fitted to each other like spoons.

He picked up on the first ring.

CHAPTER 8 . . .

The Country Store was on the first floor of a low brick building that stood between a library and a firehouse on a busy street. As though signaling their arrival, the fire siren began to wail as Charles pulled up, and a fire engine came racketing out, men clinging to it like flies to a bowl of honey.

Ella was thrilled. "Look, look!" She rolled down the window. "Hold tight!" she screamed.

One of the firemen waved. Ella waved back.

An auspicious beginning, Lois thought. Perhaps this would be easier than she had expected. Perhaps Ella would be intrigued by the new setting, new faces, and a chance to show what she could do. Perhaps she would welcome the opportunity to make friends and be part of a group functioning at her own level.

Her thoughts leaped ahead. She saw Ella getting up promptly each morning with no urging, eager to start the day. She saw herself driving Ella here, dropping her off—or no, even better, the center bus would pick her up. Ella would wait for the bus just as Ned and Amy used to wait for the yellow school bus. Would Ella pack a lunch? Perhaps they made their own at the store.

These pleasant contemplations came to a halt when she and Charles got out of the car but Ella refused to budge.

"I thought we were going to see the store?" Charles asked.

Ella slid down in the front seat, covering her face with her hands. She was wearing gloves that had belonged to Fay. "Mama's," she had confided to Charles, and stroked his cheeks with her gloved hands as though to convey Fay's essence.

"Well, *I'm* going, anyway," Lois said with enthusiasm. "Come on, Ella!"

Ella slumped down farther.

"Don't you want to see what's in the store?"

Ella shook her head.

"Okay," Charles said. "We'll be inside if you want us. Come on, Lois." He took her arm.

"But—"

"Just for a minute," he murmured, urging Lois forward. "Don't look back."

The store looked like any bakery. Pies, cookies, and cakes were set out on shelves and in display cases. A small pink-cheeked woman smiled to herself as she arranged a tray of muffins. Her eyes lit up when she saw Lois and Charles. "Special today is . . . is"— her hands performed a kind of arabesque—"blueberry muffins!" she finished, triumphantly. Another woman, plump in a cotton print dress, stood behind the cash register. Her lips moved silently as she fingered the keys.

A spindly young man in wire-rimmed glasses came through the arch at the rear of the store and greeted them breezily. "I'm Roy Starling."

The director. Not what Lois had pictured. For one thing, he didn't seem much older than Ned.

They were expected. Mrs. Corry had been in touch.

"Ella's still out in the car, I'm afraid," Lois said. "She—"

"Is that Ella?"

They turned to see her standing outside, peering in, her face flattened against the glass door. They waited. After a moment she opened the door and came in slowly.

"Glad to meet you, Ella." Roy put out his hand. Ella put her hands behind her back and edged close to Charles. "That's Mary Figlia there, waiting on customers. Ginny Belton's taking cash. Everyone takes a turn in the store. The rest of the time is spent back here."

They followed him through the arch to the kitchen, Ella trailing at a distance.

"Smells good," Charles said.

Roy flashed a smile. "Play your cards right, you might get a sample."

He introduced them to the staff. There were five staff members and nineteen clients. Besides making goods for the bakery, clients also did contract work for the city schools.

He led them to one of the long worktables. "Over here, Nan's making goodies for a school meeting."

Ella clutched Charles's hand and stared at Nan. Then she pointed. "What's it?"

"Brownies," Roy told her.

Ella frowned. "This." She stepped forward and touched Nan's head. Nan brushed her hand away as though it were a gnat and went on working.

"That's a hairnet. Would you like one?"

Ella nodded.

Irma Hale, one of the staff, brought Ella a hairnet and helped her put it on. Lois got out her compact mirror so that Ella could see how she looked. Ella gazed in the mirror. For the first time she seemed faintly pleased.

Farther along, they watched a man lining up rows of cookies on a baking tray.

"Too close," Ella told him severely. He gave her an impassive glance and went on working. "Silly!" she scolded, and lost interest.

She released Charles's hand and wandered over to a woman who was pouring sugar into a bowl of sliced apples. "Wrong," Ella told her loudly. "Brown sugar! *Brown!*" She swiped at the bowl and knocked it over. The woman gave a cry of distress as apples and sugar slopped to the floor. The man working beside her threw up his hands and brayed with laughter.

Ella smirked and edged over to Charles. Lois began to apologize.

"Not to worry," Roy said. "Bill, help Trudy clean up, will you? Ella, there's something here I'd like you to see." He led the way to where three women were making sandwiches for vending machines. "Would you like to try?"

Ella looked nervously at Charles, then at Lois.

"Go ahead," Charles urged.

"You know how to do that," Lois said. "You're good at sandwiches."

One of the women gave Ella a gap-toothed smile. "It's easy, honey."

Ella ignored her and went over to the sink, where she stood gazing at a man scrubbing pots.

Lois went to take another look at the store. Two customers were in there now. One had obviously been there before; he joked and chatted with Mary Figlia as he bought cookies. The other was a woman with two small children carrying library books; they bought blueberry muffins. It took a while to bag the cookies and muffins, it took a little longer than usual to take money and make change, but that was the only difference, Lois thought. Here and in the kitchen was a functioning community. And Ella could be part of it. There was nothing here beyond her reach, if she would only try.

Lois returned to the kitchen in time to see Ella give the man at the sink a violent shove. A pot crashed deafeningly to the floor.

"That's not nice!" the man shouted, and burst into tears.
Ella clapped her hands over her ears and bolted.

· · ·

All the way home Ella wept. In the house she threw herself on the
kitchen floor, still sobbing.

"Get up, Ella, for heaven's sake. At least wipe your nose!" Lois
proffered a tissue, which Ella ignored.

"Bad people!" Ella wailed, between sobs. "Bad!"

"No, Ella." For once Charles sounded discouraged. "It takes
time to get used to each other, that's all. Come on, get up. Show
me how to make lunch. What'll I make?"

He looked tired. Why not? Lois herself felt tired to death from
the constant effort of mentally pulling and pushing at Ella, waiting
for Ella, waiting on Ella, figuring out what would appeal to Ella.

Charles took cans from the closet. "Mushroom? Tomato?"

"No soup!" Ella shrieked. She sat up. Her hairnet had slipped
over her forehead; her nose badly needed wiping.

Charles sighed. "What, then?"

Taking her time, Ella got to her feet. Then she went to the
closet and took out a can of tuna. Breathing heavily, she took
celery and mayonnaise from the refrigerator. "I'll do," she muttered.

"Here." He held out a tissue.

She took no notice.

"Take it!" His voice was sharp.

She gave him a sly look, as though calculating how far she
could go, then sniggered.

"*Take it!*"

Her eyes widened. Slowly she reached for the tissue.

"*Use it!*"

She used it, not very effectively. Lois averted her eyes.

In silence they sat down to eat. Ella drank her milk noisily.

"Don't slurp," Lois snapped.

Ella's lower lip quivered.

No, please, not another tantrum! Lois stared out the window, refusing to see the milk dribbling down Ella's chin. Outside, it had grown colder, a wind lashed the branches of the maple, but her mind's eye imposed a different scene—the bakery with its sugary offerings, the kitchen with its warmth and activity. She heard Mary Figlia's snorts of laughter as the man buying cookies kidded her. She saw Ginny Belton slowly counting out money, tongue stuck out to aid concentration. She saw those three women chatting as they made sandwiches; one was describing a television movie, and Roz, a young, frizzy-haired staff member, joined in the talk. It was a good place, far better than she'd expected.

Charles's voice brought her back. He'd like to go shopping this afternoon, he said. He had brought no clothes for cooler weather; he needed a few things.

"Will you come with me, Ella?"

"Huh?" Her mouth fell ajar.

"Come to the store? Help me choose a sweater?"

"Store?" She looked frightened. "No! Bad people!"

"No, not there. A different store. To buy a sweater."

She took a bite of her sandwich and chewed ruminatively. "Okey-dokey," she mumbled.

Hallelujah, a respite.

"While you're gone, I'll go home. There are some things I have to take care of. In case you get back before I do"—should she actually give him a key to this house?—"I'll leave my number next to the phone. And . . . you'd better have a key."

"Take your time, there's no need to rush back. Ella and I can fend for ourselves."

· · ·

They had gone. Lois herself was about to leave when the telephone rang. It was Diane.

"Lois, I'm sorry, but I have to stay over one more night. Tomorrow, though, without fail, I'll—What?"

"I said no problem. What time tomorrow?"

"Four forty-five."

"Shall we meet you?"

"That would be nice. Or I could take a cab."

"We'll meet you. Ella likes to go to the airport. By the way, someone called here for you. I gave him the number there. I hope that's all right."

"Yes, fine. Er—how's everything going?"

"Some good news, some bad. Ella's been accepted in the work program." She gave the details and described The Country Store.

"It sounds ideal."

"Yes. But the bad news is, Ella lit out of there at a fast run today. She may refuse to go back."

"But at least we know we're on the right track. You've accomplished a lot, from the sound of it."

Listening, Lois felt more hopeful. It was true, they could hardly expect instant success; this was going to take time. She thought of the woman Irma had pointed out—heavy, with ferrety eyes and short gray hair. "That's Audrey," Irma said. "When she first came here six months ago, all she did was sit on the floor and tear up bread." But now, while Lois and Irma watched, Audrey poured batter into baking pans, then carried the pans to the end of the room and slid them efficiently into the oven.

"You're right," Lois said. "We'll just have to keep trying."

•　　•　　•

She got in her car, started to turn on the ignition, then paused. Would this seem too soon, too quick? It had only been last night. . . . If she had something, some excuse, some reason, such as the photograph—

An idea came.

She left the car and went back into the house. Upstairs, in Fay's bureau, she found what she wanted: a scarf of heavy silk, deep gold with a pattern of russet leaves.

She put the scarf in her purse, left the house, and drove away.

She found the place easily, a modest stucco house with a brick walk leading to the door. The small front garden was well planned and well kept, with white and purple chrysanthemums edging the walk. Still seated in the car, she glanced in the rearview mirror and ran a comb through her hair. Then, before her resolve could weaken, she left the car and went up the walk, mentally rehearsing the words she would use, the casual tone. *I was just passing by, thought I'd see whether . . .*

As soon as she rang the doorbell, her courage evaporated. Not that it mattered—no one came to the door. Relief and disappointment mingled in equal parts as she turned to leave.

Just then the door opened.

"Lois! What a pleasant surprise!" He sounded surprised, yes, but there was also a note of genuine welcome. For a moment she recalled her grudging politeness when she'd greeted him the previous evening. "Did you ring? Sorry, I didn't hear, the music's going."

Bohème, was it? Yes, there went Rodolfo. *Una donna!* And Mimi, timid. *Di grazia, mi s'è spento . . .*

"I was just—I just happened to be—is this an inconvenient—"

"No, not at all. Come in, come in!" She stepped inside. "How did you know I was goofing off today?"

"But—isn't the shop closed—?"

"Mondays. This is Tuesday."

She felt her face turn red. How could she have made such a stupid mistake? It showed the state of mind she was in.

"Here, give me your coat." He hung it in the closet. "I was in the shop this morning. For my first two appointments, everything was fine. Suddenly—no hot water! Something's wrong with the pipes. They're working on it now, but it's going to take a while. So I canceled the rest of the day's appointments, thought I'd catch up on things around here. . . ."

He looked different in that flannel shirt, that cardigan sweater. Older. Was it the cardigan? No pendants, no chains. From where she stood, she could see through an archway into the living room. Orange sofa and chairs, blue shag carpet, an empty birdcage. Framed photographs on the mantel.

The music poured forth.

"As a matter of fact, I was just about to make some lunch. You'll join me?"

"Thank you, I've just—"

"A sandwich, that's all."

"Well—" In fact, she had eaten very little. Ella's behavior hadn't been conducive to appetite. "Thank you, that would be nice."

She followed him into the kitchen, where the music issued from a tape player on the counter. He turned the volume down slightly so they could talk.

"May I help?"

"Sit down, relax, make yourself comfortable."

She sat down at the dinette table and looked around. The small, tidy kitchen with red-painted walls and spatter-style linoleum had the snugness of a ship's cabin, cozy and warm. A little too warm, perhaps. Gordon liked the house cool, and she had grown used to that.

"You don't mind eating in the kitchen, Lois? Fay and I always ate in here. Or occasionally—" He broke off and turned to the business of making lunch, deftly slicing and spreading. "Mustard? Mayonnaise? A little onion? No?" On the ring finger of his right hand he wore a heavy silver ring set with turquoise that looked as though it came from the Southwest.

He put the sandwiches on plates, then got out glasses.

"A little *vino*, Lois?" He held the bottle poised.

"Oh, I don't think—" On the other hand, why not? "Perhaps just a little."

Fay must have sat here just as she was sitting here now, in this very chair, perhaps. Listening to music, this kind of music. Personally, she didn't care for opera. Excessive, overblown, all that posturing and bravado. The librettos were absurd, redeemed only by being sung in euphonious Italian or French. How else could you not scoff at such lines as "What a noble heart!" or "It's been a long time since he received his just income."

Surely Fay must have associated opera with Charles, from the years when he'd played with the opera orchestra? But if there were negative associations, they must have been dispelled by Mario's arrival.

"I'm making coffee. How do you take it?"

"Just black, thank you. By the way"—she reached for her purse—"I've brought you something. It's why I came, really." She produced the scarf and watched his face change. "You gave this to Mother, didn't you? I know she liked it, she wore it often. I thought you might like to have it. As a keepsake."

For a moment he held it, his hand crushing the gold silk. "Thank you, Lois, I'm very glad to have it." He cleared his throat. "Nice of you to think of it." He replaced the scarf carefully in the tissue paper in which she'd wrapped it, then sat down to eat.

Lois remarked that the house seemed very comfortable. "How long have you lived here?"

"About fifteen years." Before Fay died, he'd been thinking of doing some remodeling, he said. "But now . . ." He cleared his throat again. "Excuse me, Lois."

Lois sipped her wine. "I like your garden. Do you take care of it yourself?"

"Yes. My dad taught me a lot about that. He was a fine gardener, an artist of the garden. . . ."

He and Fay must have sat here often like this, eating, talking, listening. But not all the time.

Suddenly she was intensely curious about the rest of this house, other rooms where Fay had been. She stood up. "Mario, where's the bathroom, please?" If there was one down here, she was out of luck.

The bathroom was upstairs.

She looked at everything, the blue-and-white-striped towels, the wallpaper printed with tiny sailboats, the striped plastic shower curtain, the long, narrow bathtub. Fay had always preferred tubs to showers.

From up here the music was quieter, but she could still hear it.

Very quietly she opened the medicine cabinet. Prescriptions, vitamins, tweezers, nothing especially intimate. As she started to close the cabinet door, a bottle of pills tumbled out with a clatter. Heart beating fast, she picked it up and put it back.

A door stood open across from the bathroom. She tiptoed in. King-sized bed, green plaid bedspread. She felt the mattress. Fairly soft. Fay had always liked soft mattresses. She gazed around. All this must have been known to Fay: the green wicker chair, the maple chest of drawers and matching nightstands, the green ceramic lamps with peach-tinted shades. Those shades would cast a flattering light. . . .

Snapshots on one of the nightstands. She leaned close to see. Fay and Mario sitting together—at a party? A restaurant? Someone's house? His arm was around her shoulders; she was smiling at him, chin raised, provocative. Wearing—was it?—yes, the silk scarf. The other picture showed Fay at the beach. Not youthful, not slender, her broad hips and generous bosom filled that one-piece black swimsuit to overflowing as she lounged on the sand, smiling, her hair tied back with a bandana. But she looked wonderful—content, replete, like a cat that's lapped up a bowl of cream and lies purring in the sun.

She could hear Rodolfo's and Mimi's voices blending exquisitely as she went back downstairs.

In the living room she studied the photos on the mantel. An

elderly couple in dark clothing gazed stiffly ahead. Mario's parents? A wedding picture showed a young red-haired bride and a groom who looked like a slimmer, younger version of Mario. This must be Mario's son. Fay had mentioned him once. And here, wrapped in a blanket, was a new-looking infant, bald, eyes closed, tiny fist aloft. And over here, in a frame, was the photo of Fay in her apron, stirring away, laughing into the camera.

"What do you think of my family?"

"Oh!" She jumped at the sound of his voice right behind her.

"Sorry, I didn't mean to scare you. That's Andrew, my brand-new grandson. Not much yet in the hair department. Spitting image of his daddy." Andy and his parents lived in New York. Phil and Sharon were both lawyers. "Between them, they do very nicely. Fine parents, too." He adjusted the angle of the frame slightly. "To see him today, you'd never know it, but when Phil was a kid, he had *molto* problems."

"Did he live with you, growing up?"

"Summers with me, the rest of the time with his mother. Kid like to drove me out of my mind, worrying. I guess you know how that is, right?" He gave her a glance. "I'm sorry, Lois. Fay was real sad for your boy. And for you, too, as I don't have to tell you. Sometimes I think they ought to put a warning on the wedding license, like on cigarettes, you know? 'Having kids may break your heart.' "

Catch this man standing dispassionately by while his son was in trouble. Catch him calmly going on with his life while his son fell off the end of the world.

"Phil wants me to move to New York. I'd see more of Andy, hear all the music I want. But it's taken me years to get the shop established. I'm not about to give it up. What would I do in New York anyway? I wouldn't want to start from square one again. And I'm sure not ready to retire at fifty-three."

Only six years younger than Gordon, but how much more vigorous and alive he seemed.

"Phil was a real fan of Fay's. He went to see her whenever he came to town. 'This is the one, Dad,' he always said. As if I needed him to tell me."

A fan? Mario's son? Mario's son visited Fay?

"Come on over here. Something I want to show you."

They sat side by side on the orange sofa, looking at the album he'd brought out. Between its pages were programs from the performances of singers—Jenny Lind, Caruso, Pons, Kipnis, Merli, Gobbi, Callas, Sutherland, Pavarotti, and more. A birthday gift from Fay. "She found these at some antique book fair. . . ."

Memory stirred. Was it four years ago, five, that time she'd stopped in at Fay's after dropping Amy off at a dance class? Fay had been working on a sizable order, lunch for forty people, a garden club. While Lois chatted, Fay went on decorating a large cake with fresh daisies. Lois mentioned that she was on her way to the antiquarian book fair being held at the college. Still carefully placing the daisies, Fay asked if there'd be anyone there who specialized in books on opera or opera memorabilia. Lois couldn't recall what she'd answered. But Fay must have gone to the book fair and found these. Not mentioning it to Lois. Perhaps because Mario wasn't yet officially on the scene. Or perhaps because she had known Lois wouldn't approve.

Why hadn't she thought to ask Fay why she was suddenly interested in opera? It might have led to some discussion about Mario. She might have learned more about him then, about the kind of person he really was. And about Fay, for that matter.

Sitting beside him now as he turned the pages, she grew more conscious every moment of his physical presence—the broadness of his chest, the slight roll of flesh around his middle pressing against the flannel shirt, the hair on the backs of his hands. She thought of those hands touching the hair of women, wielding scissors and comb while he cut and shaped, glancing thoughtfully in the mirror to appraise. His days spent on the enhancement of women, making them look beautiful, seem beautiful, even if they weren't. How would it feel to have those hands on your hair?

In the background Mimi and Rodolfo sang forth with such sweetness, such urgency, that it swept her up. Extravagant, yes, overdone, all that pathos, all that passion run amok, too lush, too rich—yet something in it reached her now.

One of the programs slipped from the album and fell to the floor. They bent simultaneously to pick it up and bumped their heads together hard.

Her ears rang, tears came to her eyes.

"My God, Lois, I almost knocked you out! What a dumb thing! Are you okay?" His hand was on hers, his voice held concern.

Absurd, colliding like that, like a scene from a Laurel and Hardy movie. She couldn't help smiling at the thought even while tears of pain ran down—the pain of the bump, the pain of Fay's death, the pain of Ned. And now, too, a pain that started in her chest and seemed to radiate downward, the pain of being here with Mario, this warm and loving man. Fay's man. In some ways Fay had been lucky.

He said softly, "Ah, Lois, don't cry," and put his arms around her.

She smelled that muskiness, mingled faintly with the smell of raw onion, and twisted toward him, pressing herself against him. A shiver ran through her as his hand smoothed her hair and he began to kiss her, deeply, fully.

CHAPTER 9 . . .

Arriving home, Lois was dismayed to see Gordon's car in the driveway. It was four-fifteen, and he had a four o'clock class, so why was he here? She didn't want to see anyone right now, especially not Gordon. More than anything, she wanted to be alone to think about the images and sounds that filled her head . . . the way they'd touched, the things they'd done, the words. . . . Never before had she been so aware of the contours of flesh, the texture of skin, the faint smell of sweat. It had seemed the most natural, inevitable act of her life, and yet the most startling. She'd astonished herself by the way she had moved, the way she'd cried out. Never with Gordon.

•   •   •

"Mr. Burke's in the study." Dora Mae's hands guided the iron skillfully over the blue oxford shirt. "Will you be here for dinner?"

"No, I'm just here for a little while. Amy wants her down jacket. I thought I'd get it packed to send off. Any calls?"

"Uh-uh. Mail's over there."

Dora Mae knew, of course, what mail Lois hoped for. She knew what Lois was really asking each time she inquired whether there'd been any calls.

Ned was three when Dora Mae had first come to work for them. Dora Mae had had a son of her own back then, Calvin, eleven. When Calvin was eighteen, he joined the army. After training, he was sent to Germany. Six months later the jeep he was riding in was involved in a three-car collision on the Autobahn. Lois and Gordon had gone to the funeral, had stood with Dora Mae, her relatives and friends, and watched as the flag-draped coffin was lowered into the grave. Calvin's father was there, but he was married to someone else by then, and Dora Mae was on her own.

She had insisted on coming back to work a few days later. "I cleared out Calvin's room, packed up his things, cleaned my whole house top to bottom," she said. "I have to work. Go clear out of my mind otherwise."

Sometime later Lois had weeded out her closet, and Dora Mae took the better discards. They wore the same size dress and shoes. "These are a higher heel than you like," Lois said, "but perhaps for church—?"

Dora Mae nodded. "I'll take 'em. Not for church, though." She packed everything up in a shopping bag. "Deacon came around asking where was I at. 'Where was the Father at,' I says, 'when he should have been lookin' out for Calvin?' "

· · ·

Dora Mae put the shirt on a hanger. "You sure look beat. Ought to get you some rest. How's Miss Ella?"

"Quite a bit better. She's started to take an interest in things, go out a little more."

"That's good. Time helps, sure enough." She unplugged the iron. "I've cooked up that chicken. Mr. Burke can have it cold if he likes."

Gordon looked up from his desk in surprise as Lois entered. "What are you doing here?"

"What are *you?*" She handed him the mail. "What happened to your class?"

"It's been switched to Fridays."

"How did things go with Leonard and Hilda?"

"Fine. We had dinner at the faculty club. I'm just as glad they had to get away promptly. I've got more than enough to do."

"Don't let me disturb you." She turned to go.

"Wait—don't rush off." He came around the desk.

"I wasn't aware you particularly wanted my company."

"There are some things we need to talk about, Lois."

"The last time we talked, you shut me up rather forcefully."

"You know why. There *are* other topics." Reproach in his voice, but also, unmistakably, a note of pleading. "You're behaving as though we're in armed camps. And now you've moved away."

"That's not fair. With Diane gone, I have an obligation—"

"That's not what I mean. You've distanced yourself, put up a wall—"

"To protect myself."

"Against *me?*" He sounded so troubled that for a moment she felt confused. He came a step closer. "We ought to be helping each other with this. I need support as much as you do."

Could this be Gordon talking? "You seem able to carry on perfectly well," she said. "Business as usual, as though nothing's wrong."

"I'm trying hard, Lois. For all our sakes. Ned's too, for that matter. If—when he comes out of this, we have to be here for him, we can't fall apart."

It made sense. Nevertheless, he was dodging the issue.

"You expect me simply to go on, then, and not think about Ned? Just forget all about him?"

"No. What I expect from you is what you, for example, expect from Ella."

"And what's that?"

"You expect Ella, rightly, to go on with her life despite her grief. Despite the fact that her mother's dead."

"That's different."

"Is it?"

"Perhaps—in a way—that's true. But what's happened with Ned is worse."

"No. Fay's dead, that's the end, it's over, finished. But wherever Ned is, whatever he's doing, he's alive, so there's hope."

Hope. For this gift of possibility, she felt a sudden spark of gratitude. "You really believe that?"

"I do. And you should, too." He put his arms around her and said, low-voiced, "I've missed you, Lois."

She was taken aback. Not like Gordon, not his style, to reveal himself as anything but self-sufficient. Moved, she clung to him. He was taut as wire; she seemed to feel every bone in his frame. Very different from Mario's fleshiness, his broad solidity. How strange that he should decide just now to let down his guard, to reveal himself as vulnerable, human. Could he possibly have guessed—? Was there something about her that betrayed where she'd been?

The whine of the vacuum cleaner began outside the study door.

He checked his watch. "Damnation, I have to go, I've got a five o'clock meeting. But you're home now—"

"No, I have to go back. Diane won't be home until tomorrow. And Charles and Ella must be back by now."

"Back from where?"

"Charles took her shopping." She nodded at his look of surprise. "It's remarkable what's happened with those two. For Ella he's the Pied Piper."

"Perhaps not so remarkable." He gathered up his papers. "He's her father, after all."

"I don't think she knows. We haven't actually explained it. I haven't, anyway. And I don't think Diane has." This is Charles, Diane had said. That was all.

"But surely he's told her?"

"I don't think so, somehow."

Charles knew he was very much on probation. He would take care, she thought, to be circumspect, to do nothing that might arouse their ire. If he explained to Ella, it might be viewed as an attempt to influence her, to sway her to his own purposes, whatever those might be.

Perhaps she and Diane should explain to Ella who Charles was. But how would they explain? Where would Ella's concept of *father* come from? People around her? Television shows? Fay certainly wouldn't have discussed it with her. Even if she had, she was hardly likely to have presented it objectively. In view of Fay's own experience as daughter, then wife, *father* was bound to be equated with wickedness, culpability, broken promises.

Suddenly, as though a curtain had risen at the theater, she saw them all as players acting out the roles in which Fay had cast them. They could make no moves, speak no lines, except as Fay assigned them. She and Diane were the avengers. Charles was the heavy, to be punished in perpetuity for his sins and for those of Fay's father.

She felt sickened. Was there no end to it?

"Gordon, what time will your meeting be over?"

"Around six."

"Then come to the house tonight, for dinner."

"You mean with all of you? Him, too?"

"Yes. I'd be curious to know what you think of him."

For herself, it was difficult to say what her feelings were by now, except that there was still a large degree of distrust. It was all very well to intrigue Diane, to bewitch Ella, to seem to want to help.

He was still nevertheless the man who had slipped out of their lives in the past as easily as a guest checks out of a hotel.

She could still remember how she had felt when it happened. . . .

She had not been completely honest with Diane about that. She had told Diane she remembered nothing, or almost nothing, but in fact her memory retained a patchwork of blurred vignettes, fragments of scenes, some more vivid than others. Now and then throughout the years something would surface. The sight of six-year-old Amy in a school play had carried her back to a time when she herself, along with other first-graders, had sung songs about Pilgrims, corn, and turkeys while her eyes searched the audience. There they were. Her mother smiled at her and gave a little nod. Her father gave a small wave of encouragement, so that all at once she raised her voice and sang louder, for him to hear.

Just the day before, as she drove to the center with Ella, the years rolled away, and she was suddenly in the backseat of another car, while Charles and Fay rode in front. Their heads and shoulders filled her view as she lay supposedly sleeping, but actually listening to the lulling sound of their voices talking quietly.

Some months back the sight of a man consoling his fallen, sobbing child had taken her back to the time she'd been running along a gravel path toward outstretched arms ready to swing her joyously, scarily, upward. All at once she'd tripped, there was blood on her knees, and she shrieked with fright, until the arms gathered her up and a voice spoke soothingly. She'd felt the bristly touch of a cheek that needed shaving and smelled the sharp, acrid odor of tobacco. . . .

She had often woken late at night to hear him playing. Lying in the dark, she had moved her hands in time to the music and pictured herself twirling, dancing, skirt flaring out like a ballerina's.

On one of those nights, angry voices sounded over the music, which stopped abruptly. The voices grew to shouts. There was suddenly a dissonant jangle from the piano, then silence. The baby woke and began to cry, mewling like a new kitten. Frightened, she, too, began to wail. Her mother came running upstairs and got her out of bed—"Get up, come on!"—then picked Diane out of her crib. Strange, frightening, in the middle of the night. She followed her mother downstairs, where the lights were so brilliant after the dark they blinded her. Then what? She remembered stumbling into his arms. He held Diane, too; she could smell the wet diaper. . . .

Then, all at once, he was gone. The music was gone, and the outstretched arms, and the sound of his voice. All that was left was a heavy silence, dark emptiness. Oh, yes. Diane had been too young to remember, Diane could find it easy to trust him. For her, Lois, it couldn't be easy; there would always be memories.

●　　●　　●

In Amy's room she found the jacket Amy had asked for. She took it downstairs and packed it for mailing, then wrote a letter to go with it.

"Dear Amy . . ." Her pen hovered like a gull waiting to swoop. "Last week, with no warning at all, your grandfather came back into our lives—"

"On my way, Mrs. Burke. See you Thursday."

"Yes. Thanks, Dora Mae."

In view of the past, I didn't exactly welcome him. But Ella has become devoted . . .

For a moment she gazed out the window at Dora Mae's straight-backed figure, in the navy coat with the squirrel collar, walking away down the road.

. . . saw your photo and asked about you . . . easier to tell him about you than it is for me to describe him to you. . . . we still

know very little about . . . helping with some plans for Ella . . .
way things are going, he may still be here when—

The pen stopped moving. Almost, her breathing stopped as an
idea came: suppose she wrote to Ned and told him about Charles.
His grandfather. He might be interested. Intrigued. Intrigued
enough to want to meet him, to—

Doubt crept in. Ned hadn't even come home to see Fay when
she was dying, so why would he be interested in Charles, a totally
unknown figure from the past?

Ah, but perhaps just that, the novelty, mystery would draw
him. Who could say? If she could bring them together, perhaps
Charles could talk to him, could somehow make him see. . . .
Look at the effect he had had on Ella. If there was even the
slightest chance, it was worth a try.

A tremor went through her.

She took a fresh sheet of paper.

Her pen moved steadily across the page. "My dear Ned . . ."

Dear Ned. Dear lost son. There must be a way. If Charles could
be the Pied Piper for Ella, perhaps he could be it for Ned, too.

CHAPTER 10 . . .

Mornings Diane typed upstairs in her room, the door closed against interruptions. "The company's prospects were still unclear back in 1907, when a youthful Walter Meldrum"—no—"when a young man from Irion, Ohio, named . . ."

Through the window, she could see Charlie and Ella raking leaves, cleaning the yard of fall detritus. "Hey, hey!" Ella shouted, scooping up an armful of crackling leaves, then tossing them to the wind with cries of delight and raking them up again.

A passion for repair and maintenance seemed to have taken hold of Charlie. He had cleaned all the storm windows and doors and installed them. He had replaced a cracked pane in the attic window, fixed a balky lock, changed the filter in the furnace, repaired a light switch in the upstairs hall. At all times Ella stood by, his eager helper, breathing heavily with self-importance as she handed him wrench, hammer, screwdriver. He was going to clean the gutters if the weather held.

Why was he bothering? Lois inquired dryly of Diane. "Only the Mahacheks will benefit from all this belated house-husbandry."

She was right, Diane thought. For a lifetime he had left all these tasks to Fay. It was a little late to be starting on chores.

But watching Ella, she could feel no bitterness, especially when she thought about that scene at the airport, Ella smoothing her new cardigan complacently over her flat breasts. "See this! New!"

"Lovely, Ella. That blue really suits you."

"And he!" Ella had pointed to Charlie, who opened his rain-coat to show his yellow sweater.

The sweaters. And dinner at the airport so that Ella could watch the planes while they ate. And flowers and wine at the house.

"He can't exactly be poverty-stricken," Diane said to Lois afterward.

Lois shrugged. "He's saving on rent, eating our food."

"Even so . . ."

"Probably his last hurrah," Lois said.

As soon as they got home from the airport, Ella sat down at the piano to demonstrate her progress. "Do, re, mi, fa, sol, la . . ." Up the scale and down, getting it right every time now, going faster, and with more assurance. As they applauded, she flashed a grin of triumph. Next she would start on a tune, Charlie promised.

•   •   •

One afternoon Diane took a break from work and went with Charlie and Ella for a ride around town. There were some places he especially wanted to see. The Adler School, to start with.

Gone, Diane told him. "They merged years ago with the university music department."

"Is the building itself gone?"

"No. It's a landmark building, they can't tear it down. But I think it's just offices now."

"I'd like to see it. On Flint Street, isn't it? There used to be a place across from it called Café Étude."

She hadn't heard of it.

They drove to Flint Street and drew up outside the building.

"It still looks exactly the same," Charlie said. "I always liked that stonework over the entrance."

There was no sign of Café Étude.

A policeman on a motorcycle pulled alongside. "No parking here, buddy. Move along."

"Buddy-move, buddy-move," Ella cried shrilly, then covered her mouth.

The policeman gave her a sharp glance, shook his head, and roared away.

They drove to Egmont Street, looking for a place called Wojak's, Wojakowski's, something like that, Charlie couldn't remember exactly, a place that sold appliances. Egmont went for miles. Charlie couldn't recall what block it was on, and they kept driving back and forth, with no success. Where Charlie thought it might have been, there was now a Korean grocery store.

What was so special about an appliance store? Diane wondered. When she asked, Charlie said he used to know someone who'd lived above the store. He started to add something further, then seemed to change his mind.

They drove across the river to the northwest side of town, looking for a place called the HiLo. Over a pool hall, Charlie said. The HiLo was gone. The pool hall was gone. The entire block had been replaced with high-rise housing.

Next they looked for a place called Esterhazy's.

"I used to play there with a band occasionally for tea dances. They fancied themselves as a kind of Palm Court, waiters serving tea and pastry while people fox-trotted. The band wore outfits out of *The Chocolate Soldier.*"

Esterhazy's was gone.

So was Reiger's.

And The Blue Parrot.

"There used to be a bar, Murphy's, down by the river."

There was still a bar, but it was now called The Watering Hole.
"I'd like to go in, just for a minute."

Diane and Ella went with him. The place was gussied up,
pseudo-Victorian, with flocked wallpaper, fake gas lamps, table-
tops of imitation marble. No one was there except a bartender,
polishing glasses.

"Sorry, folks, you're too early. Nothing happens till five."

"Is there music?"

"Sure, Kathleen plays and sings Irish songs. Sing-along every
night. Stop by later."

They drove home, stopping on the way to pick up Chinese
food for dinner. Charlie paid for it. He paid, too, for something
Ella admired as they waited for the food. "Birds! Pretty!" It was
one of those framed embroidered pictures that hang in Chinese
restaurants; this one showed a pair of cranes beneath a slender fir,
everything stitched in pink, green, and black. Under Charlie's
direction, Ella counted out the money while the proprietor waited
patiently.

"Fifteen," Charlie prompted. "One more."

"That's right, young lady, that's right!" The proprietor handed
her the picture.

Ella beamed. "Pretty! My birds!"

She clutched the picture to her bosom all the way home.

•   •   •

Lois dropped over almost daily. She would come for a short time on
her way elsewhere, or she would stay for an entire afternoon or
evening. There was something different about her lately, Diane
thought. Her attitude toward Charlie, for one thing. She wasn't
exactly warm toward him, but she was no longer virulent. She
never directly questioned him, Diane noticed, but she seemed to
be sizing him up, observing him with a watchfulness that was more
akin to interest than suspicion.

When Charlie cleaned the gutters, Gordon turned up to help,

bringing his own ladder. Lois must have suggested it. Diane was relieved. Charlie seemed spry enough for a man of his age, but she'd noticed him wince as he carried the ladder. It was nothing, he said, a touch of bursitis. "I feel it in cooler weather. I'd forgotten how quickly fall comes on here."

On their lofty perches, he and Gordon made their way diligently around the house. Afterward, as they sat down to lunch, Diane was struck by the fact that, at a quick glance, these two could almost be contemporaries, the eleven years' difference evened out by Gordon's white hair.

"Quite a job." Gordon bit into his grilled cheese sandwich with appetite.

Charlie nodded. "That spruce makes an unholy mess."

"When I was first married—to Annette, my first wife—we had a catalpa that gave us three days of beauty and nothing but work the rest of the year. Annette used to threaten to do a George Washington. . . ."

Diane was astonished. She couldn't remember ever hearing Gordon refer to the wife who had died. Before he and Lois were married, Diane's youthful imagination had been stirred by the thought of a previous woman in Gordon's past, a tragic lost love. It made Gordon seem more interesting, somehow. Back then she had questioned Lois intently. Who was she, this Annette? What had she looked like? How had she died? They had been married only three years, Lois told her; Annette had died at twenty-six, of a rare blood disease. Gordon had met her in graduate school. Her father was a noted theologian. She was very pretty, in an ethereal sort of way. Lois had seen her picture, but Gordon hardly ever spoke of her. "It was a long time ago. Anyway, Gordon doesn't like to talk about matters he considers private." Lois's tone said she approved.

Not even to you? Diane had thought.

Yet now here he was—not exactly spilling his heart out, but still. And he had met Charlie only once before, when he'd come

over for dinner. Perhaps the ritual of cleaning gutters bred a sense
of intimacy.

". . . After Swarthmore, we went to New Haven."

Annette, Swarthmore, New Haven. His life before Lois. *Life
before Lois.* Good title for a porn movie. Which was the last thing
you would ever connect with Gordon.

. . .

Diane went with Lois to visit The Country Store. She met Roy
Starling and the rest of the staff and was shown around. An idea
took shape as she talked to the staff and chatted with clients. She
was still thinking about it as she and Lois went back to the car.

"That's a good place, Lois."

"I told you." Lois fastened her seat belt.

From the store they went to visit a group home, the one Ella
would probably go to if things worked out. It was a large old frame
house, filled with light that poured in through uncurtained bay
windows; with its overhanging upper story, its porch jutting out
like a prow, it resembled a ship becalmed on a sea of lawn.

In charge were the Jacksons—Olive, a stentorian yet motherly
skipper, and Len, stolid in a plaid shirt and cloth cap, a pipe
clenched between his teeth. When Diane and Lois arrived, Len
was out in the backyard, mulching over a vegetable garden. Olive
was doing laundry. She came up from the basement to greet them
when they entered, her face shiny and red from exertion.

In the kitchen a man sat at the counter, slowly copying sentences out of a book.

"This is Rick," Olive said. "He's home today because he's had
the flu."

About thirty, high forehead, bony fingers that turned the book
toward them. *Freddy at the Seashore.* "Homework," he said, and
went back to writing.

On the kitchen windowsill stood a row of jars, each containing
a sweet potato, each jar marked with the name of its owner. In the

living room a calico cat dozed on top of the television set. From the basement came the pulsing sound of the washing machine, like a heartbeat.

Yes, Diane thought, as Olive showed them around, she could see Ella here, setting out a sweet potato, growing excited as she saw it begin to sprout. She could see Ella settled upstairs in one of the bedrooms, surrounded by things that were hers and familiar. She could picture Ella in the living room with the others, intent on the images on the screen. What would Ella make of the cat? None of them had ever had pets; Fay hadn't cared for animals.

. . .

Adam called. "How's the work going?"

"Slowly," she told him. "Always slower than one expects. What's going on in the wider world?"

"I don't know about the wider world, but I've gotten a few things done around here. I've fixed your desk lamp, the one that kept flickering. And I finally got the bathroom window unstuck."

It must have to do with the season, she thought, like hibernation or geese flying south.

"By the way, Paul called to remind us the opening's on Friday. Will you be back for the weekend?"

No, alas, though she wished she could. "It just isn't possible. . . ."

She knew what he was waiting for her to say. What stopped her from saying it? It wasn't as if she had any doubts about Adam himself, so why this reluctance to take the next step? The next logical step, in Adam's view. In most people's, even her own. She seemed to go right up to a threshold, ready—eager—to step across, when, out of nowhere, a voice warned, *Don't*. First with Michel, now with Adam.

"I have to go to Washington. When I get back—" He paused.

"Adam—" Suddenly she felt harried, pressured. "Wait just a little longer. Please. My hands are full right now."

"I'm certainly not going to force myself on you." A slight hauteur had crept into his voice—a sign of private hurt, she knew.

"Don't misunderstand. It's just—well, there's a lot going on here. Call me from Washington. Will you?"

He said he would, but his voice held a defensive distance.

She hung up, brooding. She couldn't help it, she wasn't ready, she wouldn't be pushed.

•   •   •

She and Lois began to prepare for the move in earnest. They kept a wary eye on Ella's reaction while they packed, but she no longer seemed bothered by signs of impending departure. She was beginning to let go. It wouldn't be all that difficult to get her to leave when the time came.

"We have to thank Charlie for that," Diane said.

"I guess we do." Lois taped a box shut and stood up. "There. That's the last of the linens, except for the curtains. The books are all done, and the china. What about Mother's room? Save it till last?"

"Yes. Let's tackle the basement next."

Ella and Charlie joined them in the basement. It was dingy and cobwebbed, the only part of the house that Fay had neglected. In the cavelike gloom, they studied the motley accumulation. A ratty studio couch. A console radio and record player, broken. Four ladder-back chairs. Lamps with frayed cords. A gateleg table missing a leg. An ancient manual typewriter. Shelves and shelves of jars filled with rusty nails. Dozens of cans of dried-out paint. A large adjunct freezer in which Fay had stored orders. "Thank God the Mahacheks want it," Lois said. "We'd never get it out of here."

Ella sat down on an old leather-covered hassock that had burst at the seams, and pulled at her lower lip with thumb and forefinger.

"What about these?" Charlie was examining the ladder-back chairs. One had been stripped, and a second one started but never finished. "I could work on these."

"Don't bother," Lois said. "We'll let them go as they are when we sell the furniture." She moved away. "This paint can all be thrown out."

Charlie lingered, running his hand over the back of a chair. Diane watched him. Was it he who had started stripping the chairs, all those years back? Started the job, then abandoned it, along with everything else?

"It wouldn't take much," he said. "Strip them, sand them, stain them. Ella and I could do it. How about it, Ella?"

Ella went and stood by him. She ran her hands over one of the chairs, copying him.

What on earth was the point, Diane wondered. For whom was Charlie retrieving the chairs? Never mind, it would be a good project for Ella.

● ● ●

The Mahacheks came over one evening to take measurements. Rita Mahachek, small and sleek, hurried from window to window, measuring for curtains. Her husband, George, a solid mountain of flesh, stooped with difficulty to measure the floors.

"You're taking this rug, I suppose?" Rita Mahachek's dark eyes gazed at the Herez in the dining room.

"Yes, but we're selling some of the furniture."

"Thank you, no." She raised an imperious hand. "For me, contemporary makes a stronger statement."

From room to room she scurried, her husband laboring after her, till everything was measured, noted, recorded.

Somehow, the house no longer felt the same after that. Diane felt like a tenant living in borrowed space. It was time to leave— more than time. She wanted to be back in New York, in her own place, with the unstuck window, the working lamp. It was time to put her own life in order, set some priorities.

All at once, she longed to see Adam. If she had known where to reach him just then, she would have called and told him to come as soon as he could.

·   ·   ·

But when he telephoned two days later, she was again unsure. She was upstairs writing when he called. Charlie and Ella had gone out. Lois was downstairs, making a list of furniture and other items they intended to keep and another of items to be disposed of. When the telephone rang, Lois picked up.

"It's for you, Diane," she called.

It could be Jake. Or someone else. If it was Adam, she would have to tell him—what? Come ahead? Don't come? Panic swept over her.

"I can't leave this right now. Would you take a message, please?"

When she went downstairs a few minutes later, Lois gave her a slip of paper with Adam's name and a number.

"Did it sound urgent?"

"No. He said to call whenever it's convenient."

Diane sighed and slumped into a chair.

"Problems?" Lois asked.

"Not really." She took out a cigarette. "I have to make a decision, that's all." All!

Lois seemed about to say something, but instead she pushed forward an ashtray. "I thought he sounded rather charming." Her tone was quizzical.

"Oh, yes. More than that." She lit up, then blew out the match. "If I got married, he'd be the one."

"Oh? I'm surprised to hear you'd contemplate something so conventional as marriage."

Sarcastic? Perhaps. But lacking her former tone of disparagement. In fact, Diane detected a note of genuine interest. There was no doubt about it—Lois seemed definitely more human these days, softer around the edges.

"I'm not sure yet. You'd recommend it, I suppose?"

"How can I say? I've never set eyes on the man."

"No—I mean marriage. You're in favor, obviously."

Lois shrugged. "Some of the time."

The tone was light, but was there something wrong there? Lately there'd been indications that things weren't going so well at home. All the time spent over here, for one thing. Was it Ned? A situation like that could certainly strain a marriage. Adversity was supposed to draw people together, but it didn't always work that way.

Some years back Diane had seen a drowning. A child had been caught in the current and swept out to sea. A terrible silence had settled over the watching crowd of vacationers on the beach as a Coast Guard boat brought the body in. Someone in the crowd approached the anguished parents: "We'll pray to the Lord—" "Fuck the Lord!" the mother screamed. Sounding shocked, her husband said, "Hush, Carol!" but she shook off his encircling arm and moved away. Afterward the two of them walked away separately, on opposite sides of the road that led from the beach to the parking lot. The sheriff tried to get them to go in his car, calling first to one, then the other, driving at a snail's pace. The man finally got in the car, but the woman continued alone.

"It seems strange to see you undecided," Lois said. "About anything. You always seemed to know exactly what you wanted."

Diane was taken aback. "That's how I've always felt about *you*."

Lois shrugged. "I used to think I knew what I wanted. I used to be satisfied with what I was, what I had. Lately I've begun to feel less sure."

Not necessarily a bad thing, Diane thought. Self-satisfaction wasn't the most appealing quality. Personally she preferred this new Lois, less judgmental, less—well, smug. Though, of course, it was harder on Lois.

There was something physically different, too. For the first time she studied Lois closely.

"You've lost weight, Lo. Are you trying to?"

"Not especially." She glanced down at herself, seeming not much interested. Her new slimness ought to have suited her, but her face looked pinched around the mouth and nostrils.

"Are you feeling all right? You look a little peaked, as Mother would say." Would have said.

"I'm fine. Not sleeping terribly well, that's all."

"Is it Ned?"

"So what else is new?" Her tone was falsely flippant.

Was Gordon any help with this? Diane wondered. Never mind still opening the car door for her after all these years of living together. "What does Gordon think?" she asked, cautiously.

Lois shrugged. "Keep hoping, he says. But he doesn't come up with anything concrete."

Poor Lois. Poor Gordon, too. What did Lois expect him to do, anyway? What could anyone do?

"I've been thinking . . ." Lois moved her hands as though trying to get a tangible grip on something that eluded her. "Suppose I went to see Ned, and Charles went with me? Perhaps he could talk Ned into coming home."

"Charlie?" She was astonished that Lois would think of turning to Charlie as a source of help, with this or anything else. On the other hand, it was understandable, in a way. Look at the effect Charlie had had on Ella. And not only on Ella—what about Gordon the other day? And she, Diane, too, telling him all about herself, including her long-ago *Strings* phase. "My late, unlamented poetry period." She'd smiled, self-mocking, but her voice had been tinged with regret. For failure? For not measuring up? For having missed something, she didn't know what? "Still, you tried," Charlie said. "The tragedy is never to try, to grow old thinking, What if . . . ? That would be worst of all."

Only later had she realized what he was actually saying. But at the time she'd been thinking only of herself, her past misjudgment, and the crossroads at which she had arrived. She had almost told him then about Adam. She had mentioned Adam earlier, but only in connection with music, referring to him casually as a friend who had introduced her to jazz.

"Have you asked him, Lois? Charlie, I mean. To go with you."

"Yes. I told him all about Ned, the whole situation, where he is, what he's doing. Or not doing, would be more accurate."

"But Ned hasn't listened to anyone else. What makes you think he would listen to Charlie?"

"I thought he might be intrigued, curious. Charles is his grandfather, after all. All the interest nowadays in roots, the past, people thinking about where they came from, who they came from . . ." She began to sound more sure of herself as she hurried along. "I thought, if he could persuade Ned to come home for a while, for Thanksgiving anyway, with the holiday atmosphere, all of us around, and Amy—and Charles, too, of course, he'd be the main attraction—Ned might decide to stay." Her cheeks were flushed; she looked like someone confessing illicit passion. "Charles keeps saying he wants to know his grandchildren. At first I didn't see why I should give him that pleasure. But now, yes, let him know them. Let him help save one of them."

CHAPTER

11 • • •

From above came the sound of rocking, like a furious child pounding a drum, *Won't! Won't! Won't!*

"What happened?" Lois demanded.

Charlie sat down before answering. He kept seeing flashes off to the side, like flashbulbs popping. Nothing serious, just age. But his shoulder hurt. And he'd slept poorly the night before, and the lack of sleep was dragging him down. Right now he felt like a tire from which the air was slowly escaping. "She wouldn't even get out of the car, Lois."

"Did you try—"

"I tried everything."

"We can't just give up!"

"Be reasonable, Lo." Diane spoke quietly. As though a soft voice could turn away the wrath that simmered in Lois like a pot about to boil over. "How many times can we—"

"All right, you take her on then! You take care of her!"

Like this, she was Fay come to life, face mottled as blood churned to the surface, voice coarsened with bile. It all came back to him now like a bad dream, the lurch in the stomach at the onset of battle, voices rising, words flailing.

"Maybe *you've* given up," Lois cried, "but I don't intend . . ."

On the thin edge, he thought. Because of the boy. Telling him about it, she had run on and on like a river in flood, about the kind of child Ned had been, the kind of father Gordon was, the kind of girl Karen was. On and on, about Ned and the girl, always together, so much in love. . .

He hadn't needed to say a word; that rushing torrent didn't even allow it. But he'd broken in once to ask a question: did she have any idea what had caused the breakup between Ned and Karen?

She had shaken her head, then paused, as though reconsidering. There was something Karen's mother had mentioned when she'd run into her downtown shortly before the breakup. Karen had developed a new interest, her mother reported; she had switched her major, was now very much involved in the theater department, and was talking seriously about an acting career. "Can you believe my shy little girl's talking about being an actress, of all things?"

As a matter of fact, Lois could, she told Charlie, because she had noticed on Ned and Karen's last visit home that Karen was no longer such a shy little girl; she talked a good deal more and held definite opinions. Her appearance had changed, too; she had really become quite striking-looking.

On and on, about the times she and Gordon had gone to see Ned. . . About the visits she now made to Ned on her own. . .

Finally Charlie had agreed to go with her. He said he would do whatever he could to help, though privately he didn't feel optimistic. What made her think that producing him like a rabbit from the family hat would work some magic? Still, it couldn't hurt to try; things couldn't get any worse, to judge by what she said. It sounded as though drugs might be involved, though not necessarily the cause. Whatever, the boy clearly needed help—medical attention of some kind. But as soon as he started to suggest this, Lois said sharply, "There's nothing wrong with Ned mentally."

"But from what you say, it sounds as though he might have had some kind of—" *Breakdown* was the word he'd been about to use, but she interrupted.

"You've never talked to Ned, you've never even met him, so how can you judge?" Her voice had risen. "Ned's as bright, as normal as anyone!"

This appeared to be dangerous ground. He tried another tack: what did Gordon think should be done?

"Gordon?" Her voice hardened. "Gordon's the kind of person who accepts things as they are." More's the pity, said her tone.

Would she like him to take it up with Gordon?

She shook her head. "He'll think I've put you up to it. It would only make things worse."

She was probably right. Anyway, Gordon obviously wasn't the type to spill out his heart about personal problems. He was by no means a villain, though. He and Lois probably fit quite well—or would fit well—without this kind of strain.

He felt obliged to ask one more question: what had Lois told Ned about him?

"That you're a musician. That you've been helping us with Ella—"

That wasn't what he meant. What he meant was: did Ned know about the past? From her or Diane? Or from Fay?

"Not from Mother, I'm sure. But when Ned was—oh, about ten or eleven, he once asked me about you. I told him you and Mother had been divorced a very long time ago. When I was younger than he was."

Was that all?

She hesitated. "I told him not to mention you in front of Fay. I said it would be painful for her, it would make her sad. Well, after

all"—her tone grew defensive—"you can't really expect to have
been described as some sort of admirable patriarch!"

"Of course not. But given that, given the past, Ned's not going
to put much stock in what I say, is he? Will he even believe I'm
really part of the family? Coming out of nowhere, suddenly?"

Lois insisted that she wanted him to try, anyway. "If we can
just get him home for the holiday," she kept saying. "Once he's
home, with all of us, he's bound to feel better, he'll—" She broke
off. "Gordon says I'm hysterical. Why wouldn't I be? I see my son
going right down the drain, and no one lifting a finger to stop it."
She bent her head and wept messily, like a child, not bothering to
wipe away the tears.

Charlie's heart twisted with pity. He placed a hand over hers.
"I'll talk to him, Lois. I'll do my best. But you mustn't count on it.
I don't think there's really much chance—"

"I know. But we'll try, anyway." As though in spite of herself,
her palm turned upward and she clasped his hand as though she
were drowning.

●   ●   ●

"For God's sake, Ella, stop!" Lois shrieked at the ceiling.

"Take it easy, Lo," Dianne murmured.

Charlie sat up straight. "In case we have to give up on Ella
working in the program—"

"We can't!"

"We may have to, Lois." For a second he felt a spurt of sympathy for Gordon. "If we do, I'd like to make another suggestion."

"Which is—?" Her entire demeanor said she was ready to
dismiss his idea instantly, whatever it might be.

"I'd like to take Ella back with me," he said.

You'd have thought he'd begun to speak in tongues, the way
they stared. So different, these two, one stretched tight as a snare,
the other fine-tuned but lighter, easier. And Ella upstairs, rocking

away like a furious metronome, the only one of the three who
needed him.

· · ·

Need.

His own need all those years ago. Not for love. He hadn't been
looking for love when he left. He'd been looking for—what? What
all the kids talked about nowadays: himself. And not only the kids.
Today you heard fifty-year-olds singing that tune: I'm looking for
myself, my identity, my reason for being.

Thirty-two years since he'd first wandered into the Alhambra.
The Alhambra Hotel, it was called back then, a small wooden
structure with a nine-by-twelve lobby, a few rooms upstairs, a bar.
Empty lots out back and the green of the fertile valley stretching
off to the mountains. He'd been in California for a while by then.
Getting by. Floating. But the music was getting better. Or rather,
he was getting better at it, though in most places the crowd was
busier with talk or drink or a pickup than listening. So long as
there were a few, or even just one, who actually listened. Like
that man in Dinty's in Sacramento. "That 'Georgia' was remarkable! Those breaks in the second chorus!" He was a physician
who ran a jazz society, and he hired Charlie on the spot for a
private party.

A gig in Stockton had fallen through, and a horn player
Charlie knew had mentioned the Alhambra, in Redmond, a small
town still pretty much off the beaten track.

"A couple named Sullivan runs the place. The old lady goes for
music. No great shakes, but it's worth a try if you're out that way."

When he'd walked into the Alhambra that day, there was a
woman behind the desk, talking on the telephone. He waited.
When she hung up, he told her he was a piano player looking for
work.

She gave him a thoughtful look. "We're set for the next two
weeks." Her voice was gravelly, not unpleasant. She had a curlicue

mouth and wavy red hair and seemed about forty. "You going to be around?"

"If I get work."

"Well, let's hear you. What's your name?"

"Charlie Hazzard."

"I'm Marlene Sullivan."

She led the way to the bar, where, at two in the afternoon, half a dozen customers sat on stools watching television. She nodded at the man seated at the end. "That's Pat, my husband."

Pat turned. "What's up?" He was beefy and genial, about fifty-five.

"Charlie's a piano player, Pat. He's looking for work. I'll take care of it."

Pat turned back to the television, where there was a boxing match accompanied by a loud-voiced commentator.

Charlie sat down at the piano. Marlene sat down nearby at one of the small, empty tables. "Turn that down a little, Pat," she called.

He began with a pensive "As Time Goes By," modulating in the second chorus, sped lightning-fast through "Get Happy," with a romping stride left hand, then threaded his way into "Satin Doll," lightly embellishing the melody.

A couple of the customers stopped watching television and turned around to listen.

When he finished, she said nothing for a moment. Then she asked him whether he knew "Body and Soul."

He played it for her, tenderly, building into a gentle swinging tempo midway.

At the end, she said, "Okay," stubbed out her cigarette, and beckoned him out to the lobby. As they left, Pat turned up the volume on the television.

"I like the way you play," she said. "But I promised the job to someone else for the next two weeks, and I keep my word. If you're still around after that, I'll take you on for the rest of the month."

He was very low on funds. "Is there some other place near here where I might pick up work in the meantime?"

She looked at him, considering. "Tell you what—Pat could use some help around here. He looks hefty, but he has back trouble and other problems, can't do what he used to. We'll pay something and give you room and board, if you want to make yourself useful. The rooms upstairs need a coat of paint. The outside needs some work, too."

He hesitated. He hadn't planned on being a handyman. He'd already done some of that out of sheer necessity, and he wasn't eager to do it again. But the thought of staying put for a while appealed to him. And she would probably let him use the piano during the day.

Also, there was something he liked about this woman. She seemed direct, shrewd, no-nonsense. You'd know where you stood with her. He liked the way she was keeping her commitment to the musician she'd already hired. People double-booked all the time and then canceled. And he liked the fact that she was married and her husband was on the scene. He hadn't been living like a monk, but the last thing he wanted was involvement with someone he worked for.

"It's a deal."

He stayed there and worked, painting, repairing, occasionally spelling Pat at the bar. He ate most of his meals with Marlene and Pat. Marlene cooked, after a fashion. She didn't like to cook, she didn't have much use for any domestic chores, though she did what had to be done around there, with assistance from a woman who came in to clean.

At the end of two weeks he stopped being the handyman and became the entertainment. He played six nights a week, nine till one, later on Fridays and Saturdays. Quite a few customers commented favorably. Marlene asked him to stay another six weeks, and he did. His playing was definitely catching on. People were coming back a second and third time for the music. On weekends the place began to fill up at nine, and by ten it was crowded with customers who paid attention.

Toward the end of the six weeks Marlene asked him to stay on for an unspecified period. "We'll see how it goes," she said. If he stayed, they'd increase the money and give him a better room, larger, looking out toward the valley instead of over the street in front.

He'd given some advance thought to what his answer might be if she asked him to stay. Now he tried it. "How about a percentage?"

"Maybe," she said, after a second. "Let's talk it over. Pat, too."

They talked.

He stayed.

Marlene ran an ad in the paper:

THE ALHAMBRA PRESENTS FOR YOUR LISTENING PLEASURE
CHARLIE HAZZARD AT THE PIANO

He woke up one day to realize he'd been there for six months. The arrangement suited him down to the ground. His daily needs were provided. He had no cares, not even the responsibility of cooking his own meals or maintaining an apartment. Best of all, for the first time since he'd started playing jazz, he could play what he wanted every night, with no one telling him to accommodate the customers or keep it low so people could talk. And gradually he was building up a following. The beginning of the week was always slow, but from Thursdays on, the place was packed.

The six months became a year.

A year later Pat died. Besides back trouble, he'd had a problem with his kidneys, which drinking hadn't helped.

After the funeral Marlene closed the place for a week. Charlie wondered privately whether she was going to sell. Living there, he'd been able to set aside some money, but not a lot. If he wanted to put in any kind of bid, he would have to get a loan.

He thought about it for a week, then two.

But when he finally broached the subject, Marlene shook her head. "No, Charlie. This is more than a business to me. It's my place, my home." She paused. "If you're interested, though, we might work something out. A partnership. If you can swing it with the bank."

He didn't hesitate. "You're on."

She smiled. "I'm glad you've given it lengthy thought. Let's shake on it." She held out her hand.

He took it between both of his. "We can do better than that."

• • •

It was never a marriage in the official sense. He didn't even think it was love, to start with. There was sexual attraction, but never the all-absorbing passion there had been in the beginning with Fay. But as time passed and they built the place up and began to enjoy the fruits of their efforts, something grew between them that he felt deserved the term *love.*

They shared the satisfaction of seeing the place take off. It was his music that increasingly brought people in, night after night. But it was Marlene who saw the larger picture. When she heard about the new highway coming through, she saw right away what their next move should be. "We should pick up those lots out back and build on. Twenty units to start, and a pool."

They added the units, put in the pool, and enlarged the bar to a lounge that accommodated a hundred and fifty.

Within two years, everything was paid for, the units were constantly occupied, and the lounge did a steady business.

Most of the time, Charlie played solo, but occasionally he led a trio, adding bass and drums. Listeners now included not only people from the area and towns down the line but travelers as well. A writer for a leading jazz publication came through on his way to the Monterey Jazz Festival and wrote them up: "You don't often find good music in a motel setting, but at the Alhambra in

161

Redmond, pianist Charlie Hazzard delivers sounds that are swinging and mellow." Not a rave exactly, but a tip of the hat that Charlie enjoyed. And it didn't hurt business.

Over the years, they again enlarged the lounge and added more units and a coffee shop and dining room. The days when Marlene had cooked and cleaned were long over; they had a full-time staff now, and a manager, Ed Ramirez, whose wife, Sonia, was in charge of housekeeping.

. . .

One day Charlie and Marlene sat down to go over some business with Ed. First item on the list was Bo Tandy. Bo, the head cook, had been coming in drunk and getting into fights. He'd been warned half a dozen times. Should they let him go or give him one more chance? Next, Sonia was going to need some extra help, with Memorial Day coming up; two more full-time maids and two or three part-timers should do it. Next, what about those quotes for new floor covering in the older units. . .

They discussed all this and more over lunch in the dining room, lunch being abalone and a salad that made you think twice about giving Bo his marching papers.

Afterward Marlene and Charlie took a dip in the pool, then stayed out there for a while. Marlene read for half an hour—she went through at least two mysteries a week—and then lay back and drowsed off. Meanwhile, Charlie gave some thought to what he'd play that night. Friday, four sets. An Ellington medley. And what else? "How High the Moon." "I'll Be Around." "Violets For Your Furs," a great Matt Dennis song with a beautiful verse and inventive melody, one of Marlene's favorites. Something by Monk. "Straight, No Chaser." Did he have a sheet on that? And there was something of his own, an idea he'd been working on, a tune in a minor key with a Latin feel. . . . He'd try it out, see how it went. . . .

The sun was getting to him. He lay back and closed his eyes. He heard voices, people in the pool calling to each other. The sound of music floated out faintly from the bar. Lee, the bartender, had put on a tape, "Blues In the Night," Charlie Hazzard at the piano. Harold Arlen, you couldn't get better than that. Great Mercer lyric, too.

A feeling of total contentment swept over him.

He opened his eyes. Marlene was reading again. He watched her. Fifty-four and she'd gained a few pounds, but she wore them well. The sunlight caught the coppery red of her hair, which she kept that way with a little help; nowadays she wore it short and curly, and it suited her. An attractive woman, and what was more, a first-rate woman. How had he ever been so lucky? Something like fear ran through him when he thought how easily he could have missed all this—Marlene, his music, this life. Soon they would go indoors and up to their apartment and make love, not wildly like kids, but taking their time, aware of each other's needs and desires. Familiarity took away a certain edge, but it added something, too: the comfort and assurance a traveler feels on returning to a country where he's often been before, where he speaks the language fluently and knows his way around.

Marlene glanced up. "What? Did you say something?"

Smiling, he shook his head.

· · ·

On some occasions Charlie hired a group to play for a holiday or for times when he and Marlene took off. They were beginning to travel. They went to Hawaii, Australia, and Japan. They celebrated Marlene's fifty-fifth birthday on the *QE2* going to Europe. Aeons before, in another time, another life, Charlie had run into a party of Europeans when he'd played at the HiLo, a dinky place over a pool hall—the kind of place that had given Fay fits. They were Swedes, design engineers, in Shelburne to consult with a machine tool company. They were the best listeners he had ever had back then, knowledgeable, enthusiastic; they told him everyone in Sweden was crazy about jazz, he must go there someday. So now, besides England, France, and Italy, he and Marlene went to Sweden, Norway, and Denmark.

Whenever he looked back, he was always thankful they had taken time to do these things before Marlene became ill. They had three years after she was diagnosed. Sometime during the second year he stopped smoking and struck a bargain with a Providence he'd never believed in that if Marlene beat this, he would never smoke again.

Halfway through the third year Marlene went into the hospital for surgery. A week later she begged Charlie to take her home again. The doctors were annoyed. She belonged in the hospital, they said. He said: why? Would they cure her? Would they lengthen her life in any meaningful way? They said no, it was too late for that, but they could make her comfortable, could do what needed to be done. He said, "I'll make her comfortable. I'll do what needs to be done." He learned how to give injections and change dressings. He hired nurses to take care of her at night, but days he took care of her himself. In fine weather they stayed outside. She was now shadow-thin and often cold, so he kept a blanket tucked over her as she lay in the sunshine. Against the gray of her skin, the artificial red of her hair looked ghastly, almost clownlike. Her voice had lost its gravelly timbre; it was as thin and frail as the rest of her. On cool days they stayed indoors and played gin rummy or watched television or listened to records. Marlene liked vocals, and they spent hours listening to Billie Holiday, Sarah Vaughan, Jeri Southern. Evenings, if she felt well enough, Charlie and Ed Ramirez would set her up at a table in the crowded lounge, and she'd stay there for a set or two while Charlie played. If someone else was playing, Charlie would take over for a set and play her favorites.

●   ●   ●

For a month after Marlene died, he didn't touch the piano. He sat in the bar every night and drank until Ed got him out of there and up to bed.

Finally, as though at a signal, he stopped drinking and started playing again. And he threw himself into hard physical labor. He ordered structural improvements and landscaping and did some of the work himself. He added an exercise room for guests and used it daily. He couldn't seem to concentrate on paperwork, so he delegated some of the office tasks and handled a shift at the front desk.

By now he could have retired if he wanted. He'd had attractive offers from chain operations to buy him out, but he wasn't interested. He wasn't about to go adventuring or make a fresh start in his late sixties. Nor was he ready to roll over and play dead. He would stay where he was, go on as he had. The Alhambra was just what he needed.

He was in good health. Apart from his shoulder, he had only one problem: since Marlene's death, he slept poorly unless he took pills. Even with pills, his rest was fragmented, filled with dreams that seemed like movie previews. Or postviews. Marlene, the time he'd auditioned, while Pat watched boxing on television. Her excitement as they'd boarded the ship for Europe. The fight they'd had when she'd accused him of sleeping with a singer he'd hired. (He hadn't, though in truth she'd caught his eye.)

And, for the first time, there were replays from his former life . . . Fay standing a drowsy Lois before him, holding the squalling baby out, reminders of where his duty lay . . . Diane in a sagging diaper, beginning to crawl, a pixie child with a gummy smile . . .

He woke from these dreams with a sense of loss so strong he felt as though he'd had a limb amputated. Part of it was Marlene, of course; he missed her badly. But that wasn't all of it.

He began to think more and more about his former life. What had happened to the children? Lois, Diane, and . . . ? Once he even got as far as the telephone and called directory assistance, but there was nothing listed for a Fay Hazzard, or for a Lois or Diane. No Hazzards. Fay must have moved or remarried. By now she'd be—he had to think—sixty-one, sixty-two?

An idea came: he sent for a subscription to the Shelburne newspaper. He read every issue cover to cover when it arrived.

There, fourteen months later, he came across the obituary. "Fay Hazzard, after a brief illness." Still at the same address. "Owned and operated Continental Catering . . ."

The final sentence told him what he wanted to know: "Survived by three daughters."

•   •   •

Strange, the way they'd assumed he wanted something when he first arrived. Yet the more he thought about it, the more he had to admit they were right, in a way. Was he too late for what he wanted? "To every thing there is a season." Everything in life depended on timing.

They probably thought his offer to take Ella was prompted by remorse. Not so. In taking her—if they'd let him—he'd be filling a deep need of his own. Could he make them understand that? Should he try? Not now. No need to bother with that right now. Now, while Ella's tattoo rattled the ceiling, he simply gave them some facts.

He told them about the Alhambra, to start with. "A hundred and forty units, pool, tennis courts. There's a dining room and a coffee shop. . . ." It was important for Ella to have an occupation. "She could make sandwiches for the coffee shop. Or salads and desserts for the dining room, whatever. Or she could work outdoors. Does she like to do that?"

"She's never done it, that I know of. Has she, Lois?"

Diane still looked amazed, but at least she appeared to have grasped his words, whereas Lois still seemed stunned, uncomprehending. Diane would always be quicker than Lois, about everything. Not that Lois was stupid, but Diane was more intuitive, ready to go with her instinct. And flexible, she bent with the wind. If Lois had just a little more of that, this business of the boy might not be hitting her quite so hard.

"Whatever, it would be up to Ella. As the spirit moves her. There'd be plenty of people around for her. I'd be there all the time. . . ."

Besides the Alhambra, he had other assets and investments. Real estate. Stock. He'd recently built a recording studio just off the bar, for the big names who played there, recording on the Alhambra label. "I won't make a killing, it's really more of a hobby. Before coming here, I stopped in New York to see a distributor—" He stopped, seeing that Lois finally wanted to speak.

"How do we know all this is true?"

"I can give you names, references, financial statements. Better still, come see for yourself. I'd like you to visit."

. . .

Lois had gone home. Ella was asleep. He and Diane were talking.

It was more like a catechism. He hoped it wouldn't go on much longer. It was now eleven-thirty, and this had been a full day. He was too tired to think very clearly. And his shoulder hurt.

"You weren't actually married?"

"In a ceremony? No."

"Children?"

"No."

In the circle of light cast by the lamp, Diane's face took on a pearly sheen. "You came back because you were alone, then?"

He hesitated. "Not exactly."

He didn't say so, but he needn't have stayed alone. He could have had all the company he wanted after Marlene died. He knew a lot of people. There were women he saw from time to time. He could have married if he wanted.

She leaned forward, intent. "Why, then?"

He felt impaled by her gaze, like a moth on a pin. Here was his chance to give his side of it.

But wait, he'd got it wrong: she'd asked why he'd returned, not why he'd left.

For a second he closed his eyes. His head seemed top-heavy, as though it might fall off. "It's been a long day, Diane. Could we adjourn? Tomorrow, I promise—"

She glanced at her watch. "Good heavens, I'm sorry, I didn't realize—"

He hauled himself to his feet.

She stood up and moved toward him, putting out a hand as though to help. "Do you feel all right?"

He pushed a smile through lips that felt like boards. "Tired, that's all."

Outside, a car flashed by. Shadows rushed like a dark flood over the curtains, then receded.

CHAPTER 12 . . . .

Seated in Lois's tasteful earth-toned living room, Diane resisted the temptation to disarrange the magazines aligned on the coffee table. Instead she slipped off her shoes and stretched out on the sofa, where down pillows oozed comfort.

Comfort. Lois looked as if she could use some. She moved about the room constantly while she talked, as though she couldn't bear to sit still. "We should get on with what we started to do. Ella should have an independent life, with peers."

"Lois, there was no choice before. But now . . ." She spread her hands. "He's her father. He has some special feeling for her. And we know how she feels about *him*. Should we just ignore that? Do we have the right to rob her of that?"

Lois halted by the French windows. "Could we trust Ella with him?"

"Trust . . . ?"

"She'll be quite different on a permanent basis. A real handful. Then what? He hasn't exactly shown staying qualities in the past, so far as we were concerned."

Diane was silent, considering. "I felt trapped," he had told

169

her. "Weighed down." She had thought: do I get it from him then?

"But, Lois, all those years afterward, spent in one place, with one woman . . ."

His partner—and wife, too, never mind the legalities. Playing his music, yes, but also taking responsibility, caring for her, in every sense, to the end. Listening to him, Diane had felt a deep hurt, a stabbing jealousy on her mother's behalf. With effort, she had forced her mind away, turned the talk instead to the time when he and Fay had still been together, and happy.

"Yes, happy at first," he'd said. "Loving at first."

"Then what happened? What went wrong?"

He'd taken a long moment to answer. "She was opposed to what I wanted to do. Very strong, determined."

"Nothing wrong with strength," Diane retorted.

"That depends. Turned against you, it can be lethal."

She'd bristled. But his words suddenly revived the memory of long-ago struggles. Lois resisting a singing career. That exchange in the kitchen after the wedding, Fay's crushing grip on Diane's arms until—as always—she had given her mother the answer she wanted. For though she'd loved Fay, she had always been a little afraid of her. She had complied with her wishes in order to please and to avoid the battles she could only lose. "Yes," she had said, constantly. "All right. I will. *Okay!*" And Fay had switched the lion's share of love to the daughter who seemed to offer obedience. More obedience, anyway, than she got from Lois, a rebel in those days.

. . .

A rebel? *Lois?*

Diane stared across the room at her sister. How could she have missed it all these years? As her weapon, Lois had ultimately used a conventional choice, but it had been, nevertheless, a declaration of independence. Independence from Fay, at any rate.

She saw it now, oh, yes. As their mother must have seen it, too, all those years ago. Must have recognized, too, the double implications of Lois's choice, knowing what—who—Gordon, nearly twenty years older than Lois, stood for. It was ironic, because Gordon was probably a good choice for Lois. Not exactly scintillating but with sterling qualities, as the phrase went. Ballast. Lois needed that.

Feelings of remorse, of shame, swept over her as the picture grew indisputably clear: she'd been the one who was spineless, currying favor, while Lois was the one who'd shown some backbone. Yet all these years she had misjudged Lois, given her no credit.

Lois, I'm sorry.

She didn't realize she had said it aloud until Lois, looking startled, said, "No need for that. You're entitled to your opinion." She came and sat down at the end of the sofa, leaving space between them. But at least they were no longer talking across the room. "We have to be very careful about this, Diane."

"I agree. But he's changed, Lois. He isn't the man he was when he left."

He wasn't the only one, Diane reflected. Fay, too, had changed over the years. Fay had been difficult, domineering, a shrew— Diane didn't need Charlie to tell her that. But Fay had also been spirited, gallant, loving. Later especially. And Mario attested to it. All of it was true; nothing was simple.

"Changed? Yes, he's older," Lois said. "Which means there's something else to consider. His age. Suppose Ella went there, then he died?"

"She'd come back, that's all."

"Then where are we? Back to square one. We'd have to begin all over again, trying to get her into a program. We should do that now, while he's here to help. Otherwise it's only a short-term solution. We'd just be substituting him for Mother."

"No. Being with Charlie would be very different from being with Mother," Diane said.

"How?"

"When Ella was with Mother, she was only with Mother, she didn't do anything except help Mother. With Charlie, she'd be out in the world, mixing with people, working with people—"

"The motel help?"

"Among others. Why not?"

Lois didn't answer immediately. Her fingers locked around a shallow bowl that stood on the coffee table—a lovely thing, Diane thought, with its simple glaze of grays and browns. "How do you think Mother would feel if she knew?" Lois asked.

"The point is, she loved Ella. She'd want her to be cared for, happy."

"With him?"

Diane said, wearily, "She won't know, Lois." Why must Lois persist with this . . . vendetta? As though she were carrying a sacred flame, sworn to see it never extinguished. "Anyway"—dare she say it?—"is it really all quite so black and white? Everything that happened?"

● ● ●

"Don't try to tell me it was all Mother's fault," she had warned. "Two children, another on the way. Alone days and nights, uncertain finances. And you, the man she married, turning into someone else—not at all the person she bargained for. Then vanishing, with never a word or visit or—"

"That's not true." Charlie's voice was matter-of-fact, as though the truth needed no emphasis. "For a long time I wrote. I called. I sent money. But Fay kept me away from you, intercepted my letters, broke all contact. . . ."

The words seemed to reverberate.

Could it be true? she wondered, as he went on talking. How could she tell? By now how could anyone judge the rights and wrongs of all that had happened? There probably was no one true answer.

"God knows I'm not blameless," he said. "Far from it. I made the wrong choice—"

"In leaving?"

"In getting married when I did. To anyone."

She thought sadly, There are no clear-cut villains here, only mistakes, bad luck, the stars colliding. The wrong choice. Wherever there was choice, there was bound to be risk. But who could get through life without choosing? *Living may be dangerous to your health.* Who'd said that? Adam, that time he'd been trying to persuade her . . .

Suddenly she found herself aching to know what Adam would think of Charlie. And vice versa.

⚫   ⚫   ⚫

Lately she had also been wondering what Adam and Fay would have thought of each other if they'd met. Would Fay have taken the same attitude toward him as she'd taken toward Gordon when Lois had first announced she was getting married?

There were two reasons why she had never brought Adam to meet Fay. One was that Adam might misinterpret this, thinking that she—Diane—was taking their relationship to another level. The other reason was that she hadn't wanted to get into a quarrel with Fay about Adam. She had always taken care never to mention to Fay any man in whom she was really interested. Occasionally she had referred to some casual acquaintance, but she always took pains to make it implicitly clear that this was unimportant, nothing lasting.

Once, however, when she was seeing Michel, she had mentioned his name too often. Fay had glanced up from a menu she was studying. "It sounds as though you're seeing a lot of this man. This—Michel."

"Oh . . ." Diane shrugged. "Michel's fun to be with, that's all, a good talker, good dancer." She was careful not to speak of him again.

After Adam had moved in and things seemed to be going so well, she began to wonder how she would break the news to Fay if she and Adam—But then she'd stopped worrying. No point in crossing that bridge unless and until she came to it. Then, all at once, Fay was gone, and the difficult prospect no longer existed.

But why *difficult?* she wondered now. Why should she have been afraid to tell Fay she'd found someone she loved, someone with whom she wished to share her life? Shouldn't her mother— any mother—be glad to see her daughter embrace the chance of happiness with a loved and loving partner? Shouldn't Fay have been pleased to see the family grow, to welcome a son-in-law? Especially someone like Adam. Fay would have enjoyed Adam's charm, his intelligence, his wit. And Adam would have enjoyed knowing Fay, if Fay had ever let him really know her. What a pity, what a waste, a missed opportunity.

• • •

"So where do we stand?" Lois asked.

"I've been thinking. . . . Suppose we take a trip out there? See for ourselves what it's like, what the situation would be. Perhaps we'd take Ella along. See how that goes."

Lois seemed to reflect. "That's not a bad idea."

They discussed it. Lois had been to California several times with Gordon, to meetings, but she didn't know it well. Diane had been there only once, to San Francisco on a job.

Lois went and got a map. Together they studied it.

"We'd rent a car, I suppose, and drive up from San Francisco. I wonder how far it is to Redmond?"

"Less than a hundred miles, I think," Diane said. "We'll have to ask Charlie."

"Imagine Ella on a plane!"

They looked at each other, wondering. Ella had never been on a plane; she had rarely been out of Shelburne.

"And seeing the sights! Such excitement!" Diane said. Not

only for Ella. She felt a sudden quickening at the thought of this trip, a journey of discovery, filling in the blanks, completing the picture.

"I wish Mother had talked to us more."

"About what?" Lois folded up the map.

"About what happened between her and Charlie."

Lois gave her a strange look. "I thought perhaps she had told you things she hadn't told me."

"What made you think so?"

"The two of you were close. She confided in you. I was never part of that. I'd come in and hear the two of you talking together, laughing together. As soon as I appeared, you'd both stop. You never explained, you never included me."

"That's not so!" Diane was shocked. "It was just that— Well, you married and left. But I was still at home, still company for her, so—"

"Never mind. It doesn't matter."

"Lois—"

"It's not important." She looked away. "I suppose no one ever hurts their children intentionally."

Children. The greatest risk of all, surely. Yet twice, deliberately, Lois had chosen it. How was it she, Diane, had always thought of herself as the risk taker?

Now, feeling uneasy, discomfited, she was the one who stood and wandered. She came to rest by the piano, where photographs stood banked on the polished wood. There was one of Amy she hadn't seen before, Amy on a sailboat, smiling buoyantly. An attractive, likable child, Amy. Amazing how she had stayed unspoiled despite all the attention lavished on her, especially lately. In the past Diane had tended toward partiality for Ned. Moody and introspective, Ned had always seemed more interesting.

A pang went through her.

That time she'd gone to visit, something about him reminded her of a turtle that had lost its protective shell. Lois's fears were probably justified: he seemed to have become a street person. Looked like one, anyway, with that unkempt hair that could have used washing, that torn windbreaker and dirty jeans and, more than anything, that air of aimlessness and general neglect, which seemed even more marked in someone of his age. Still, he wasn't getting into trouble or breaking any law. And she hadn't seen any actual evidence of drugs, though there were other things she'd felt concerned about . . . the way he'd sounded, for example, his voice flat and listless, without affect—until he talked about Karen. Then he grew agitated, excitable, tripping over words in his haste to get them out. Listening, she'd felt chilled.

She could certainly understand why Lois was upset. But in some respects Lois seemed almost as irrational as Ned, the way she kept blaming Gordon and Karen by turns. And now she seemed to be pinning all her hopes on Charlie.

Lois's hands kept turning the bowl on the coffee table, inch by inch.

"Where did you get that?"

Lois looked up. "Get what?"

"That bowl."

Her hands fell away. She sat back abruptly, as though she'd been reproved. "It's one of mine."

"Yours? You mean, you made it?"

Lois nodded.

Had Lois told her—? She couldn't remember.

"It's beautiful, Lo. Is all your work as good as this?"

Lois smiled faintly. "When did you stop beating your wife?"

"Where do you work?"

"I share a studio downtown with Marge Norris."

"Do you show? Sell?"

"This was in the Long Lakes show. I sell some. Not exactly in volume."

"Could I see your studio?"

Lois nodded. "Sometime. Tomorrow, if you like."

Diane thought: I've never really bothered to get to know her. She felt a stab of regret for having missed something, having been negligent.

CHAPTER 13 • • •

Through the darkness, red digits warned five twenty-one, five twenty-two, five twenty-three . . . Lois closed her eyes, willing herself back to oblivion.

No use.

At six o'clock she got out of bed, moving quietly so as not to wake Gordon, and stood at the window, watching snow twist lazily down through the early light. First snow of the season, just a flurry, one of those paperweight snow scenes, a ten-second shower of artificial flakes. Leaning forward, she pressed her forehead against the coolness of the glass. *The North wind doth blow and we shall have snow, and what will poor Ned do then, poor thing?*

Lying awake, she had played and replayed the sound of Ned's voice on the telephone. Tuesday? Okay. Twelve o'clock? Okay. Completely indifferent. Asked where he'd like to meet, he couldn't seem to come up with anything. They'd finally settled on a place where they'd met in the past, basically a pizza parlor, with a jukebox. She would have preferred a quieter spot where it would be easier to talk, but Ned wasn't being any help. He hardly seemed to be paying attention.

"Good!" She'd made her voice briskly cheerful. "The Chalk-
board, then, at noon. Your grandfather's really looking forward to
meeting you, Ned."

He didn't say he was looking forward to seeing her or to
meeting Charles; he made no response at all. Never mind, this
much had gone as she'd hoped.

Dora Mae had come in then and found her weeping. "Mrs.
Burke, what's the matter? Is it Ned? Is he sick? Or—hurt, some
way?"

Some way. "Ned's all right. It's just—" She couldn't seem to
stop crying.

Dora Mae went swiftly out and came back. "Drink that down,
won't do you a bit of harm." She dispensed tissues. "One of these
days, that boy's gonna come to his senses, you'll see. Remember,
he's around. When a person's around, there's always a chance,
right?"

Nodding, she wept harder, as much for Dora Mae as for herself.

•   •   •

She had told Gordon that she was going to see Ned and that
Charles was going with her. But she had said nothing about her
hope that Charles would be able to persuade Ned to come home.

Gordon had walked in the other day as she was gathering some
things to take along: Ned's sleeping bag, a sweater, a book on river
rafting. He flipped through a few pages of the book. "What's the
point of this? Ned's no longer interested." He sounded dejected.

"I thought it might remind him of that trip you took together."
A trip down the Salmon River, their gift to Ned for his fifteenth
birthday. "It can't hurt to remind him of happier times."

Gordon turned another page. "You're going on Tuesday, did
you say?"

She held her breath. Was he about to propose coming along?
This was one time she didn't want him along. If her plan was to
succeed, the atmosphere must be as harmonious as possible. The

last thing she wanted was Gordon's upsetting Ned with challenging questions or remarks about his appearance. But she needn't have worried; he let the matter drop.

. . .

By the time she and Gordon sat down to breakfast, the snow had stopped and started several times. A light scattering lay on the ground like a sprinkling of dandruff. With an eye to the weather, she had put on a warm tweed suit and a high-necked sweater. Just as well Charles had thought to buy himself gloves the other day. Did Ned have gloves? She must remember to take some along.

Gordon opened the newspaper. "Looks as though it means business out there. Couldn't you put this off for a day or two?"

"It's all arranged now, Gordon." She buttered a piece of toast.

He turned a page. "Are you driving, or is Charles?"

"I am." Charles had offered to drive, but her car was more comfortable for a trip out of town, and anyway, she liked to drive; it was always satisfying to watch the car eat up the miles, to feel the engine's quick response to her touch. "Are you ready for—*Damn.*" The coffeepot slipped in her grasp.

Gordon helped mop up.

"Try again?" She held out the pot and forced a smile.

He moved his cup toward her. "You'll take it easy, driving?"

"There's nothing wrong with my driving, Gordon."

"But you know how seeing Ned affects you."

With effort, she held still. She mustn't get into an argument—not now. Anyway, it was true, the prospect of seeing Ned did affect her. How could it not? And Gordon's tone hadn't been critical or hectoring. Solicitous, rather. In fact, things had somewhat eased between them lately. On the surface, at least. Gordon still wouldn't discuss the problem of Ned, but he was willing to talk amicably about other matters, safe subjects. Amy, for example, coming home tomorrow, thank heaven. Ella. Charles and his proposal.

Gordon had been as astonished as she was about that. But he hadn't been surprised to hear that Charles was solvent. "What made you think otherwise?"

She shrugged. "His timing, I suppose—turning up when he did. And the way he cadged a room. He doesn't look especially affluent, does he?"

"He doesn't look especially like a pauper, either."

Gordon favored the idea of a trip west to—as he put it—scout the territory. "You're right, Lois, there's much to be said for Ella's staying here and becoming self-sufficient. But there's also a case to be made for her being with her father."

She thought, he *would* say that, he'd be relieved to get Ella off their hands. Then she felt ashamed. Gordon might have no particular love for Ella, but he wouldn't advocate one course over another just to suit his own convenience.

It helped, talking this over with Gordon. About most things, Gordon could be extremely helpful, logically weighing pros and cons. It was only with Ned that he wouldn't be helpful, wouldn't take any active role. But she was resigned now to the fact that she could expect no help from that quarter. So be it. She would have to solve the problem on her own, that was all. Since she'd made that decision, her resentment toward Gordon had somewhat lessened. A few nights before, they had actually made love, Gordon in his usual fashion, careful, respectful, almost polite, while she herself had been—oh, not the way she'd been with Mario, all-giving, without limits or restraints, but somewhat . . . freer than usual. Gordon had seemed so pleased afterward that she had felt a reciprocal warmth, mixed with pity for the fact that he didn't seem to realize how much more was possible.

How much more . . .

Every time she thought about that, about Mario, she grew almost sick with desire. In the almost six weeks that had passed since her visit, she had heard nothing from him. Again and again, split nearly in two between longing and fear, she had started to dial his number. Half a dozen times she had gotten in her car and started to drive to his house. But fear had won out every time. No, not fear. Sanity. She mustn't go back there. In any case, he hadn't suggested it; he'd made no reference to seeing her again. But perhaps he would call. If he called, then what? If he called, she would say—she would tell him—oh, who knew what she would say, what words might actually come from her lips if he called?

Meanwhile, her time with Mario had taken on the aspect of a fevered dream, an erotic fantasy that had never really happened . . . except for one moment that had come to seem more real than all the rest—the moment when, as she lay there afterward, with Mario's hand resting casually on her hip, her glance had fallen on that photograph of Fay. Fay watching her, watching them, smiling at them, laughing. Laughing at them. At her.

Mario had followed her gaze. "Relax, Lois, it's no big deal."

No big deal. Did he mean that Fay wouldn't have minded? Or did he mean that he himself didn't attach much importance—? All in a day's work, was that it?

For him, perhaps. Not for her. For her it had been epoch-making, for more than one reason. She had learned something today about herself that could never be unlearned: who would have dreamed that she could so easily throw discretion, restraint, control to the winds? The thought was astounding, and also frightening, for who knew where such recklessness might lead? A murky vista opened before her, a yawning chasm of unthinkable consequences from which she recoiled.

The other thing she'd learned was that, like it or not, she had more in common with Fay than she'd realized: she and her mother shared a taste for passion—not to mention a taste for the same partner. The thought was in some ways distasteful, yet something about it didn't entirely displease her. If Fay had still been alive, she might just possibly have asked her about it. Not directly, of course—it was hardly the sort of thing you could ask your own mother—but in a roundabout way. And from the manner in which Fay answered, even if it wasn't an outright answer, Lois might have learned what she wanted to know. The two of them might have ended up talking together confidentially, like friends, talking together and laughing, the way Fay used to with Diane.

•   •   •

She had arranged to pick Charles up at nine-thirty. She pulled up outside her mother's house just after nine-thirty and sat waiting in the car, with the engine running. Snow fell in a leisurely way; the windshield wipers moved steadily back and forth.

Come on, Charles, where are you?

She was about to go and fetch him when the door opened and he came out with Ella. Ella was wearing a coat.

Lois was appalled. Surely he wasn't proposing to bring— Then she realized that Ella was only seeing him off; she remained on the porch, watching him go. When he reached the car, he turned around and waved. Ella waved back, then patted her mouth rapidly in a gesture that meant she was blowing kisses.

Lois waved, too. Ella called something that Lois didn't catch. For a second, it looked as though she were about to follow Charles, but then Diane emerged and drew her inside. Seconds later Ella appeared at the window, waving exuberantly as they drove away.

"I hope you had a chance to have breakfast," Lois said.

"Yes, Ella and I had a fine breakfast. We were up early, working on the chairs." While he was gone, Ella was going to finish the sanding. Tonight he and Ella were going to a concert; a jazz band was playing a benefit at a local high school. "I think Ella will enjoy it."

Ella would, Lois thought; she would stamp her feet and clap her hands, like the rest of the audience. She would fit right in, be one of the crowd. It was the sort of outing that wouldn't ever have occurred to Fay, or to her and Diane. Diane was right: Charles would lead Ella to new experiences, broader horizons. Ella should probably go live with him. Once this problem of Ned was settled—which might be sooner rather than later, thanks to Charles—she and Diane would have to definitely arrange that trip to California. There were other things, too, that needed attention. With this business of Ned on her mind, she'd neglected everything. She had stopped calling friends or having people over. She no longer bothered with committee meetings or other obligations. She hadn't set foot in the Shed for weeks, had made nothing for the various pre-Christmas shows that would start after Thanksgiving.

"We'll be back by six, you said?"

"Yes, easily," Lois told him. "What time is the concert?"

"Eight o'clock."

Was Diane going with them?

No, Diane was expecting a friend from New York, Charles said. "Which reminds me, Diane said to tell you he'll be staying awhile. Add one more for Thanksgiving dinner."

Ah, the voice on the telephone! Interesting to see what kind of man might seriously interest Diane at last.

"That's better," Charles said.

"What is?"

"You're smiling."

"Am I?" She turned and smiled directly at him.

●   ●   ●

Farther off were the hills, curving gently skyward. In the immediate vicinity the river flowed through barren-looking fields, now carpeted in white. Some lines learned in high school kept running through her head: "On either side the river lie / Long fields of barley and of rye. . . ."

What was in those fields, or would be, come spring? Neither barley nor rye. Nor did she in any way resemble the pathetic Lady of Shalott, floating along in that boat, arms folded in eternal acquiescence. Acquiescence was for Gordon; she was through with acquiescence. And with despair. For the first time she felt not only hopeful but optimistic. What a difference it made to have the promise of help, a supportive ally. A wave of gratitude swept over her.

"Are you warm enough, Charles? Shall we turn up the heat?"

"I'm fine, thanks."

· · ·

The car purred along through the bleakly empty landscape. There were no signs here of human habitation, nothing but cars and trucks roaring along the highway. Snow kept falling. Charles turned on the radio for a weather report. Too late, it had ended; music was playing. Jazz.

He adjusted the volume. "May I leave this on?"

"Of course."

She listened, too, trying to hear what he heard.

"What's that called?"

" 'Train and the River.' Jimmy Giuffre on reeds."

Yes, she could hear the whistle of a train in the music, haunting, lonely, the sound of the transient always moving on. . . .

Sadness settled over her again like a veil. Staring ahead, she caught a glimpse of shapes moving way off in a field, cows huddling together for warmth. Why weren't they in the barn? Barn, bairn, my bairn's left out of the barn. Tears threatened.

Something flashed black and silver against the frowning sky. Was it—? Yes, a rough-legged hawk plummeting down, after a mouse probably. Up he flew again now with his hapless prize, heading for the hills.

If she could only scoop Ned up and carry him home like that. She saw the neighbors pouring from their houses. *Look! Up in the sky! It's a bird! It's a plane! No, it's Supermother!*

She laughed aloud and felt better.

"Let me in on it?"

Still laughing, she shook her head. "It's really too silly to explain."

The music was interrupted by a weather bulletin. Temperatures were heading for the low thirties. Three to four inches of wet snow were predicted. Charles looked dismayed.

"This is nothing," she told him. "A nuisance, that's all." She was used to driving in this weather, she said; it happened all the time in this part of the world. Don't you remember? she nearly said, but didn't. To reassure him, she moved discreetly into the right lane and stayed there, moving steadily along, letting traffic roll by. They were making good time; there was no need to rush.

● ● ●

"I'm sorry, I'm afraid I need to make a stop," Charles said.

"So do I."

She pulled into the next rest area.

In the washroom mirror, her reflection looked different. Her pallid-looking skin had taken on some color; her eyes had lost their dullness and were now brightly gleaming.

She glanced at Charles as they settled back in the car. Unflappable, he seemed. Reassuring, that calm demeanor. Warming, the clasp of his hand that time, the comfort of human contact and sympathy. How good it felt to have him along.

For a moment she forced herself to conjure up Fay, to imagine what her mother would have felt if she'd known. But for once nothing came, no acrimonious thoughts, no dutiful surge of hatred. Instead there was a kind of—loosening. With relief, she finally relinquished a legacy that could only perpetuate grief and rancor. No more. She might mourn always for the years that were gone, the memory of loss, the time when her world had tilted off axis, but the man who sat beside her now was no longer an enemy.

● ● ●

A trailer hurtled by, spraying slush. The windshield wipers worked nonstop.

"We're nearly there, Charles, just another ten miles. Let's run through what we're going to say to Ned."

"Lois"—he shifted in his seat—"I don't much like the idea of an advance scenario. Let's just take it as it comes. Better to be as— well, as spontaneous and natural as we can."

"Goodness!" she said lightly. "You make it sound as though I'm plotting some kind of wicked coup."

"No, that's—"

"It makes sense to plan ahead, doesn't it? This isn't going to work unless we choose our words carefully."

"No matter what words we choose, Lois, this may not work. I did point that out."

What was this?

"Are you telling me"—her voice grew shrill with incredulity— "are you saying we should give up? Before we've even tried?"

"No, Lois. I said I'd do my best. But frankly I think there's very little chance—"

"I'll be the judge of that!" Her hands tightened on the wheel until her knuckles showed white.

"Even if we can get him to come home, what then? You can't lock him up. You can't make him follow orders."

"I'll make him see—"

"With the best will in the world, Lois, there are some things we can't control. Don't you see—"

Oh, she saw all right! She felt sick with disillusion. He had promised. He had really seemed to want to help. And now . . . Let it go, he was saying. Like Gordon. Let everything go, includ- ing Ned.

"All right, you've had your say. It's my turn now." Tears blinded her. "You do whatever you like, I'll handle this myself! You needn't say a word to Ned! Ned's nothing to you, after all—"

A truck thundered by, horn shrieking.

"Lois, calm down! Watch—"

"Your own children were nothing to you! I should have known—"

"*Lois—!*"

The car swerved crazily, leaped, hit.

Somewhere in the farthest distance, someone screamed.

· · ·

With enormous effort, she opened her eyes. The steering wheel was poised above her. Through it she saw an iron-colored sky.

Something lightly touched her cheek. Her nose. Her cheek. Snow. She tried to say it, "snow." But her tongue was strangely thick in her mouth, no sound came.

Slowly, with infinite care, she turned her head. It hurt so much that she lost consciousness.

When she came to, the snow had stopped. She tried to move some other part. Arm. Hand. Foot. No.

Wait—did she hear—? There'd been someone. . . . Now she remembered. Her voice strained in her throat as she tried to call: Ned! *Ned!* But all was silence.

CHAPTER 14 • • •

Jake's office had been done over. The walls were now covered in charcoal suede, there were maroon suede chairs and a pearl gray carpet. His desk was large, free-form, made of some exotic wood. Right now his feet were propped on that desk. From where Diane sat, the Chrysler Building appeared to be sprouting from the top of his head.

"Suppose I call you toward the end of January? Someone's opening a chain of gourmet food stores, wants a classy brochure, touches of French."

"Sorry, Jake, I'll be away. I'm getting married next week."

Married. Whenever she said it or even thought it, she checked cautiously for questions, doubts, twinges of regret, but none came. Occasionally she still seemed to hear Fay's voice, warning, remonstrating, but it had grown very faint, very distant. Even when she heard it, she could now talk back to it with confidence. *That's enough. I know what I'm doing.*

• • •

The last time she had heard it was the day of the move. Late that afternoon, after the movers had left, she, Gordon, and Adam had

191

gone through the house, taking care of final details: fastening the
windows, sweeping the floors, getting rid of trash, carrying out a
few fragile items that hadn't been entrusted to the movers.

Then Adam and Gordon went outside to remove the door from
an old refrigerator they'd found in the garage.

Alone, she walked through all the rooms one last time, her
footsteps resounding in the emptiness. How large the living room
seemed without the piano. For a moment she saw her mother
at the piano, heard the strains of Chopin, Liszt, Schumann.
The Romantics. Anyone less romantic than Fay would be hard to
find.

The piano was in storage; she wasn't going to sell it. So far she
had no room for it, but she was beginning to see that this might
change, and she wanted to keep the option open.

In the kitchen she stood where the table had been, then closed
her eyes and let her thoughts spin back, forming a web in which
the past was netted. Once again, she heard Fay calling as she and
Lois came home from school: "When you've taken off your things,
I could use a hand in here!" She heard Fay instructing Ella: "Now
the eggs. Careful. Measure out the flour. Level off the top, remember. Good!" She heard Fay laughing as she told some story, her
laughter loud and full-bodied, like Fay herself.

Once again, she saw Fay at Lois's wedding, smiling, gracious,
apparently resigned, wearing the blue lace dress Lois had insisted
she buy for the occasion. An awful dress, Fay thought, and Diane
agreed. "Makes me look like the dog's dinner," Fay said. They'd
giggled.

Once again, she saw Fay in her nightgown, working in here the
night after the wedding. She heard the crack as Fay's hand struck
the table. She felt the pain of Fay's iron grip on her arms. "Don't
you make the same mistake!" Same mistake, same mistake, same
mistake. . .

Adam walked in. "We're all done, Diane. Gordon's waiting in
the car."

She heard him but couldn't move.

What was that? She stared at it—the corner of something, sticking out from under the refrigerator. A card, it looked like. She bent and picked it up. A photograph, sticky, covered with dust. It looked as though it had been down there for years, fallen between the refrigerator and a cabinet that had now been taken away. Fay playing the piano, a much younger Fay. Lois at her right, Diane at her left. Lois looked about sixteen, seventeen, plumper than Diane remembered. Diane seemed about twelve—skinny white legs, hair in a ponytail. Fay was smiling at Diane, whose mouth was open wide in song. She had always sung along vigorously, if not tunefully, when Fay played songs she liked—"Hi-Lili-Hi-Lo" and "Edelweiss" and her favorite folk song, "Old Dan Tucker": "Old Dan Tucker was a mighty man, he washed his face in a frying pan, combed his hair with a wagon wheel, and died with the toothache in his heel."

"Let's hear you, Lois," Fay always urged, but Lois would only toss her head disdainfully.

She gazed at the picture.

"What was the occasion?" Adam asked.

She couldn't recall, but it had to be something special, for Fay was wearing a dress, and a bandeau across her hair. Where was Ella? Perhaps Ella had taken this picture; one of them might have adjusted the camera for her so all she had to do was snap the shutter.

Wait—was that a flower pinned to Fay's dress? Now she remembered. "It was Mother's birthday. We bought her that corsage."

The corsage had been Lois's idea; she had insisted on an orchid, a white orchid, despite the cost. Fay had exclaimed in pleasure when she saw it.

Diane and Ella had baked a Black Forest cake, Fay's favorite, and put candles on it. How many? Diane studied the picture. Clean jawline, no sag beneath the chin. Forty-one, forty-two . . .

"You don't resemble your mother."

"No, I look more like—" Her voice broke.

He said, gently, "It's time to go, love. Don't linger with the ghosts."

Time to go, yes. She put the photo in her purse. And time to let go, too. But it was going to take a while.

•　　•　　•

Jake swung his legs down and offered felicitations. "Honeymoon, huh? How long will you be gone?"

"Four weeks."

Not exactly a honeymoon, but she let it pass, taking the easy way, as Lois would say. She and Adam were going first to California, a retrospective journey before the Alhambra changed hands and many of the people who'd known Charlie were gone. She was going to talk to Ed Ramirez at length, and to Charlie's lawyer—to anyone who'd known Charlie in any way at all, musicians, friends, people who'd worked for him. It was the closest she would ever come now to filling in the picture.

"Call me when you get back," Jake said. "There might be something else on the fire by then."

She might, she might not. She had started writing an article about work programs like Ella's. One of the slicks had shown an interest. When she came back, she wanted to get on with it. She might develop it into a book, passing up the corporate jobs to work on it full-time. She could afford to do that for a while, thanks to Charlie. Thanks to Charlie, she, Lois, and Ella each had tidy nest eggs of their own.

After leaving Jake, she had nearly an hour before she was due to meet Gretchen for lunch. She decided to go to the library to look up some information she needed for the article.

In the periodicals room she filled out request slips.

"These two aren't available," the young man at the counter said. "I'll bring the others."

She looked after him as he went away, her attention caught by the shape of his head and something about his walk.

She thought: This must happen all the time to Lois. O my sister.

•　　•　　•

Lois's physical injuries hadn't been so bad, if you considered what had happened to the car. They'd had to cut her out of the wreckage. Charlie had been thrown clear, a long way clear, but his head had hit a rock. He'd died on the way to the hospital.

In time Lois would be all right, physically. She would recover from her concussion. Her fractured arm, dislocated shoulder, and broken ribs would all mend, her countless contusions and abrasions would heal and fade, and so would the cut running from the corner of her mouth to her chin. In time she would be practically as good as new, the doctor said.

But her mental state was another matter.

At first she had barely talked at all, to anyone, not even to Amy when she came to see her. She just lay in that hospital bed, her arm in a sling, her bruised face a startling purple and black. Of course, at that stage it wasn't easy for her to talk with that cut tweaking at the corner of her mouth whenever she moved her lips. Each word cost her pain.

Her friends did all the talking when they came to visit in the hospital. She must hurry and get well, they told her warmly; she was badly missed at tennis, at the swim club, at the library collections committee meetings. The new wheel she had ordered months before had finally arrived, Marge said, and Pot Luck in Ithaca wanted a dozen of her elliptical plates. Friends brought books, magazines, perfume, candy. They sent so many flowers that the hospital room resembled a florist's shop.

Even Mario, of all people, sent flowers. Which was nice of him, Diane thought, considering the way Lois had always behaved toward him. Was behaving still, as far as she could see, for when the lavish arrangement of carnations arrived and Diane read her the card, "Best wishes for a speedy recovery. Regards, Mario," Lois made a sound of disapproval—at least it sounded like disapproval—and turned her head away.

"I'll make room for them over here on the windowsill."

"No!" Diane was startled at her vehemence. It was the most animation she had shown so far. "Give them away." She spoke stiffly, moving her lips as little as possible.

"Are you sure?"

"Yes. Too many." She gestured at the laden windowsill. "Anyway"—she winced—"can't stand carnations."

Since when? Diane wondered as she carried them out. But of course, Lois had disapproved of Mario from the moment she met him. She wasn't about to change her mind because of some flowers.

Lois had been allowed to go home after just a week in the hospital on condition she kept off her feet and had someone to take care of her. With Ella, Dora Mae, and Gordon, she had all the care she needed. The fact that she needed care turned out to be a positive factor as far as Ella was concerned. Diane had talked to Ella about it in advance, explained that Lois was coming home but she wasn't all better yet, she was going to need help. Ella kept bobbing her head. "I'll help, I'll help," she kept saying, sounding pleased and proud.

She made no fuss when Diane and Gordon moved her permanently out of the house and over to Lois's. She settled in peacefully in Ned's room. His posters were still on the walls, his books were on the shelves, and so was his fossil collection from grammar school days. But now the embroidered cranes hung between a Julian Bream poster and a swimming citation. The rug from Fay's bedroom covered the floor, and on it stood Fay's bureau and rocking chair. Instead of rocking, Ella spent her time hovering over Lois, fetching and carrying, cooking dishes that might tempt her, helping her to the shower. Diane worried that Ella's constant presence, her overeager fussing, might irritate Lois or tire her. But Lois didn't seem to mind.

Whenever Lois napped, Ella sat by as if to make sure no harm would come. Did she associate Lois's present condition with Fay's final illness? Diane wondered. Lois and Fay had been in the same hospital, the one where Fay had ultimately died. Ella had visited them both there. So perhaps she was afraid that Lois, too, might. . . Not an altogether illogical fear, from Ella's point of view, after Fay, and then Charlie, had been taken from her.

●   ●   ●

Diane had dreaded telling Ella about Charlie. She'd kept putting it off, until one day, after Ella had been playing the piano, she forced herself to do it.

Ella had been going to the piano daily, first at the house, then at Lois's, to practice. Practice consisted of playing the same scale over and over, slowly and laboriously. Chinese torture, Gordon called it. As a finale, she kept plunging her hands down on the keys, producing a dreadful cacophony that she accompanied with piercing cries of "Sunny-sunny! Sunny-sunny!" Each time she heard it, Diane was again overwhelmed by a sense of loss, the second loss far worse than the long-encoded first. She tried to dissuade Ella from playing, for if she herself found this unbearably painful, how must Lois feel? But Ella wouldn't be dissuaded. Diane could only hope that Lois, still spending most of her time upstairs, would not be able to hear it and that Ella, lacking encouragement, would in time give up.

When Diane finally had her talk with Ella, Ella said nothing at first, only watched her, head lowered, peering up warily from under her eyebrows. She gave no indication that she understood.

Diane groped for further words to make it clear.

"Gone away," she said, cursing herself for ineptness. "Like . . ." She paused. "Like Mama."

Ella's expression changed slightly. She pulled at her lower lip. "In the water?"

"What?" Then she realized: Ella had seen Fay's ashes scattered. "Yes, Ella." Not exactly, but it would do. She took Ella's hand, prepared to offer consolation.

But Ella didn't weep or cry out. She kept her head bent, seeming intent on pulling off a hangnail. Had she really understood? Or was it possible that she thought Charlie had only gone away for a while on some errand?

•   •   •

Gone away.

Sometimes, watching Lois, Diane felt her heart contract with pity. At other times she could barely stop herself from shrieking reproaches. *Why did you have to drag Charlie into it?* She had to keep reminding herself that Lois was suffering. And it was an accident, after all, it could have happened to anyone, a car skidding on a snowy road.

Charlie, we never knew ye.

They never would now. All that was left were memories of several hours of talk. She felt heartsick and cheated, for Charlie and herself.

Adam would never know him now. She would never hear them talk together about music, earthquakes, fixing things. And if she ever in the future had a child of her own, she would never be able to say: Here is your grandfather, here is your grandchild.

Do you realize what you've done? she wanted to scream at Lois.

Then she would think of what Lois was going through, was likely to go through for some time to come, and the hard knob of anger would yield to compassion.

•   •   •

As time passed, Lois's injuries began to heal on schedule. She still tired very easily, and because of her damaged arm and shoulder, she wouldn't be able to use her new potter's wheel for some time. But twice a week Marge drove her to the Shed, where she could do lighter tasks for an hour or two, such as dusting and reorganizing the display—not the heavier items but cups, mugs, smaller bowls and plates.

Friends came to the house as they had to the hospital. Lois still wasn't talking very much, but she seemed to like having them around; she asked them all to come back, come often. Gordon wasn't thrilled, Diane noticed, about the number of people constantly coming and going; he shut himself in his study, emerging only when they had gone. But he raised no objections; he seemed to understand this was helpful for Lois, even necessary. Poor Gordon. This was a terrible time for him, too. She wasn't sure Lois understood that.

She had come to a new respect for Gordon. If only he would open up occasionally, wouldn't always insist on stiff-upper-lipping it. But people had to deal with trouble in their own way. Her way was the opposite of Gordon's. She still wept at the slightest reminder—a song heard on the radio or an obscure item in the paper about the citrus crop, datelined Redmond. She still talked constantly to Adam and Gretchen about what had happened. Lois was the one she most wanted to talk to, but Lois had made it clear she didn't want to talk, and Diane couldn't press her on that. Lois must be free to put herself back together the best way she could. Later she would surely want to talk and would allow Diane her own need to talk. But not now. Not yet. Perhaps not for a long time.

Only once since the accident had Lois mentioned Ned, and even then she'd said very little. She'd been home from the hospital for three weeks. Her arm was still in a sling, and her face still looked as though she'd been in a prizefight, though some of the bruises had faded to a greenish yellow.

Diane was with her in her room. Gordon was teaching, Dora Mae was doing laundry, and Ella had gone downstairs to watch television. Lois lay on the chaise by the window, reading—holding a book, anyway. Diane sat on the bed, writing a letter to Amy.

The telephone on the nightstand rang, and Diane picked up. "Hello?" No one answered. "Hello?" she said again, several times. All she heard was a click; then the line went dead.

She hung up and went back to her letter.

"Who was it?" Lois asked.

"Wrong number, I guess."

"What did they say?"

Diane glanced up. "Nothing. It was a hang-up."

"But—"

As Lois stared fixedly, Diane suddenly understood.

"Lois, no, it wasn't—" She stopped, for how, in fact, could she know?

Lois covered her face with her hand. From behind it, her voice came muffled. "I keep thinking one day I'll pick up the phone and hear his voice—or he'll write—or perhaps—just—"

Yes. Arrive out of the blue one day, like Charlie.

How long had Ned waited for them that day? Diane wondered. Had he worried when they hadn't shown up? Maybe, maybe not. Ned had other things on his mind. Perhaps he'd waited for a while, then simply wandered out again, thinking that he'd gotten the wrong day or they'd changed their minds. More likely, he'd hardly thought about it at all, had just gone on his way with that strange, lost look.

"Lois . . ." She paused. Should she tell her? She and Gordon had decided to say nothing; better not to encourage hopes that might only be dashed. But now she changed her mind. Apart from everything else, it was time Lois realized that Gordon was prepared to do all he could to make her feel better. "Gordon's going to look for Ned next week. If he finds him, he'll try to bring him back. I said I'd go along."

"Perhaps we can get him to come home to see her," Gordon

had said. "We can ask him to get in touch, at least. It'll help, won't it, if she hears from him? If he lets her know from time to time that he's—" He had taken off his glasses and rubbed his eyes. They looked pink and sore. Diane had longed to touch his hand in comfort, but everything about him said no.

Lois began to weep. Diane went and put her arms around her. But a moment later Lois pulled away. "No. Don't go after him. What's the use?"

What?

"But, Lo—I thought—I mean, just now you said—"

"We can't force him if he really doesn't want . . . He knows where we are if . . ."

Diane gazed in disbelief. It was what Gordon—all of them— had tried to tell her all along. By what kind of miracle had she finally understood? Perhaps it had something to do with having lots of time to think, first in the hospital, then at home. Or perhaps Charlie's death had in some way—? Whatever, however, thank heaven it had finally happened. For Lois's sake, and Gordon's too.

But looking at Lois's stricken face, she couldn't just leave it at that.

"I'm sure Ned will get in touch with you, Lois. Sooner or later."

She might be right about that, she might not, but she had to say it.

· · ·

After more time had passed, Diane raised the subject of Ella's going to work at The Country Store.

"It's time we got her started there, Lois."

Diane didn't say so, but Gordon had discussed this with her. When Lois started going about her life again, what was Ella going to do? he'd asked. Sit around here and twiddle her thumbs?

Gordon was right. Dora Mae, too, had begun to hint that Ella, with less and less to occupy her as Lois recovered, was getting to be a bit much.

Lois shrugged. "You think she'll go? I don't. You remember how she acted even when Ch—" She stopped.

Diane let a second pass. "Still, we should try."

"Go ahead." Lois picked up a magazine. "Good luck. You'll need it."

Diane did her best. She talked to Ella and reminded her of her visit to the store with Lois and—she used his name deliberately—Charlie. She talked about the work that was done there and reminded Ella how good she was at that kind of work and how much she enjoyed it. Throughout all this, Ella remained blankfaced and silent.

"You know where I mean, Ella? The Country Store. Where they make cakes and cookies and sandwiches."

Ella chewed hard on her thumbnail. Finally she spoke. "Where Charlie?"

"Yes, that's right."

But Ella wouldn't listen to another word, let alone agree to go back. When Diane tried to speak, she rushed to the piano and banged as hard as she could with both hands.

"No use," Diane reported to Lois. "You were right."

•   •   •

Diane's next visit was two weeks later. She arrived on a Sunday, planning to stay through Monday morning and take the afternoon flight back to New York City.

On Monday morning Ella shook her roughly awake. "Up, up!" She ripped off the covers.

"What? What is it?" Diane came slowly out of a heavy slumber. "Ella, it's not even six o'clock! What's the matter?" For a second she was afraid. Ella was jabbering away; she couldn't really follow her. Go? Go where? To the store? At this hour? To get what? What store?

"The store, silly!" Irritated, Ella stuck her face close to Diane's. "Those people!" she shouted.

Suddenly Diane understood. "Fine! Great! I'll get ready!" She leaped out of bed and hurried to dress before Ella changed her mind.

Ever since then Ella had been working. Mondays through Fridays she packed a lunch and the bus picked her up just down the road. She spent her days baking and making sandwiches, learning to read and write, do simple arithmetic, handle money.

Diane would never know what had caused her to change her mind. Was it possible that, as Adam suggested, she had gone to the store in the hope of seeing Charlie?

Over the weeks since then there'd been a noticeable change in Ella. She was talking more, sometimes in full sentences. She talked about her work, about people at the store, about sights she saw from the bus each day. She had made friends with a woman at the store named Terese. They always sat together on the bus. "There's Trees!" Ella would cry as the bus came into view and a hand waved from the bus window. "Trees and me did money," she reported. "Trees and me did egg salad sandwiches." As Ella became more socialized, she grew more tractable. And now that she was otherwise occupied, her interest in the piano gradually waned, then ceased, to everyone's relief.

There was another change, too—one that Diane and Lois both remarked upon. Ella was more cooperative, yes, and more articulate. But some natural boisterousness seemed to have left her, some playfulness of spirit, some energy that had translated into exuberance as well as temper. A good thing, too, Lois said; she was becoming less childish, more mature. True, Diane said, but—

But what?

She didn't quite know how to express it—the feeling that some quality of uniqueness had left Ella. Lines were beginning to show on her face. She had begun to seem like any tall, gaunt woman sliding into middle age.

● ● ●

Not long after Ella had started at the store, Mrs. Corry called to say the group home had a vacancy.

To Diane's surprise, Lois was in no hurry to have Ella move out.

"I don't think she's ready to venture forth alone."

"She won't be alone," Diane pointed out. "She'll be with people, with peers."

"She's with peers all day, at work."

"But—I thought Gordon wasn't happy about having her around on a long-term basis?"

"Oh, Gordon's gotten used to her. She's really no trouble."

"It would be good for her, Lois. She'd become more independent." *Don't you remember, you yourself said—*

"Maybe later," Lois said, vaguely, and changed the subject.

Let it go, for a while anyway. You couldn't push Lois about anything these days.

Diane's thoughts went back, skittering hurriedly over the recent past, to the time when Charlie had asked to take Ella. What Charlie needed, we all need, she thought. Lois, too. And Fay. Though Fay, she realized now, had used commitment to Ella as an excuse to take no further risks. She saw it all now, clear as a landscape etched by lightning.

"Try trust," Adam had pleaded. "Don't be afraid to be human, Diane. Even to seem a little weak occasionally. Goddammit!" he exploded. "If there's anything I can't stand, it's a macho woman!"

She had laughed, as he meant her to, even as she absorbed his meaning. Some lines went through her mind: "My true love hath my hart, and I have his, / By just exchange, one for the other giv'ne. / I hold his deare, and myne he cannot miss: / There never was a better bargain driv'ne."

CHAPTER 15 · · ·

A daunting January wind swept along the streets of Manhattan. When Diane looked out her window to gauge the temperature, she saw people hurrying by with their heads tucked down against the cold. It seemed a good time to be going to California.

They were booked on a three o'clock flight. Adam had gone out to an early-morning appointment, but he would be back by noon, and he had already packed. Diane had treated herself to staying in bed until nine, then had showered and eaten a leisurely breakfast. Now she was packing without haste, choosing clothes for both mild and cool weather. She would need rain gear, too, because from Redmond they were going to Portland to see Adam's parents and then to Seattle to visit Adam's older son, Matt, who was in college there. The younger one, Eric, was in college in England; they would be seeing him this summer.

They would be gone for a month in all. When they returned, they would move to their new apartment, two floors in a brownstone—huge living room, real dining room, high ceilings, tall windows, two fireplaces, great kitchen. There would be room for the piano and for that good set of dishes Lois had been keeping for her.

The phone rang continually while she was packing. Several times it was for Adam. Once it was someone who wanted her to write a script for a video presentation. For a second she was tempted. When? Right away. Sorry, not possible. Then Gretchen called to say bon voyage and went on at length about a man she'd met who seemed ideal, except for his hobby. What hobby? Free-falling. "I think you should pass, Gretchen."

One way and another there was turning out to be less time than she'd thought. So when the phone rang still again, she snatched it up and snapped "Hello" in a tone meant to discourage conversation.

"Diane? Is that you?" Lois sounded a little cowed.

"I'm sorry, Lois. Just that the phone keeps ringing and I'm trying—What's up?"

"I just wanted to mention—you will drop Ella a line, won't you?"

"Of course." Her tone was short, for Lois knew very well that she always sent Ella picture postcards, with simple messages printed on them, from wherever she went. Ella would be able to read the messages herself now; she even had a friend to show them to, if she wanted.

"The other thing is—you will take plenty of pictures? Of . . . everything?"

"We'll take lots of pictures, I promise."

"Good. I want to be sure . . ." The words trailed off.

"Lois"—her voice softened—"you should go there and see it all yourself before too long."

"I will, sometime. But I can't leave now."

"But"—should she say it or not?—"you can't spend the rest of your life—"

"I know you're in a hurry, I'd better let you go. Safe journey." She hung up.

Diane continued packing, but her thoughts were occupied

with that last exchange. Lois seemed to have picked up the reins
again, in most respects. She worked at the Shed, met friends for
lunch, attended college functions and social events with Gordon.
But much of the time, she seemed abstracted, remote—not cold or
unfriendly, but removed, out of reach, visible but untouchable, as
though enclosed in a glass bubble. Often she appeared to be
listening to something, listening for something, that no one else
could hear. *I can't leave now.* Not to go to California nor to go with
Gordon to a three-day meeting in Santa Fe. Not to go with Marge
to that craft show in Vermont. Not even to go to Parents' Weekend
at Amy's school—Gordon had finally gone to that alone, as he had
to go alone to anything that involved staying away for any time
at all.

In Shelburne the previous week Gordon had walked in while
Diane and Lois were having lunch. In the tone of one offering
good news, he made an announcement. "My book's finally done,
Lois. I'm taking a sabbatical. We'll go to Europe or—"

"No," Lois said. "Not now. Maybe later."

"Lois . . ." He paused. "Don't you think—"

"I can't. Anyway, there's Ella."

Perhaps this would be the time for Ella to move to the group
home, Gordon said. Or if that wasn't acceptable, Dora Mae was
willing to stay and keep an eye on her. He had talked to her
about it.

Lois shook her head.

Gordon shot Diane a look of appeal.

"A trip sounds like a fine idea," Diane said heartily. "A change
of scene would do you good. Both of you."

"It needn't be a long trip," Gordon said. "Two or three months.
Less, if you prefer. We could certainly use a vacation. I could,
anyway. Things around here have been pretty dreary."

"Take a vacation," Lois said politely. "Go on your own."

"You need it, too. For one thing"—his expression turned

grim—"it would help you get back some sense of perspective. I
don't know how much longer I can go on like this. How much
longer I'm willing to go on."

Lois walked out. They sat listening to the sound of her footsteps on the stairs.

Gordon removed his glasses and rubbed his eyes. "I'm sorry,
Diane. I didn't mean to subject you to this kind of scene."

She racked her brain for words that might help. "She's bound
to come around eventually, Gordon."

"Maybe." He replaced his glasses. "Meanwhile—" he
shrugged—"here we are."

There they were, yes. And there Lois seemed determined to
stay, lady in waiting. Strange that she had finally achieved a real
breakthrough in one respect yet couldn't seem to take the next
logical step and go about her life in the normal way. It was as if a
tape had jammed, then got going again, but farther along had
jammed once more.

Gordon was clearly at the end of his rope. Couldn't Lois see it?
And he'd sounded as though he meant what he said. How was Lois
going to feel if he left her?

·   ·   ·

Soon Adam came home. They ate a quick sandwich, then col-
lected their luggage and left the apartment. A cab came along. Off
they went to La Guardia.

"Feels like snow," the driver said. "Sure wish I was going on
vacation. You folks headed somewhere warm?"

She didn't listen as Adam answered. She was thinking about
the list of questions she'd made. Questions about Charlie and
about Marlene. She also had a list of things she wanted to see. First
the Alhambra, of course, and Charlie's apartment there. Charlie
and Marlene's apartment. The table in the motel dining room
where he and Marlene had had their meals. His piano. The
recording studio.

There were bound to be photographs of Charlie around. Of both of them. There would be tapes of his playing. Why hadn't she ever thought to ask him to play for her at length? The only times she'd heard him were when he'd played briefly for Ella. He'd mentioned something once about recording on his own label, the Alhambra label. Ed Ramirez would know about that, or the lawyer would know.

From various documents the lawyer had sent, she had learned what Charlie's middle initial stood for: Benjamin. Charles Benjamin Hazzard. For some inexplicable reason that seemed to tell her a lot more about him. She kept wishing that she had known this earlier. There were many things she wished that she had known earlier.

* * *

"Guess I'll take the Triborough," the driver said.

"By the way, Diane. . ." Adam's hand rested on her knee. "My mother called this morning while you were still asleep. She's managed to change her shift for the time we'll be there."

Adam's mother, Eleanor, called Ginger, had recently come out of retirement to go back to nursing. Adam's father, Toby, was a former trade unionist with memories going back to the days of the Wobblies.

She was immensely looking forward to meeting Adam's parents, to seeing who and where Adam came from. From whom, for example, did he get those Mephistophelian eyebrows? Whence came that habit of pushing up his lower lip with one finger whenever he concentrated? She would look for these in Toby and Ginger, just as she had once searched for common characteristics in Charlie and herself. She was determined that she was going to like Adam's parents; she was equally determined that they would like her, too. She wanted this for Adam's sake and her own, and for still another reason: if she and Adam should ever have a child—if she ever dared take that risk, that considerable risk—that child would have grandparents, she would make sure of that. They would visit back and forth, distance notwithstanding; they would call each other often. No matter what might happen, now or in the future, she would always take care to maintain that connection—all her connections, with Adam's family and her own. Adam. Toby. Ginger. Eric. Matt. It pleased her to add these names to the roster, to see the circle widen. In this, she supposed, she was the opposite of Fay.

• • •

They halted at a traffic signal, beside another cab. Their driver rolled down his window. "Hey, Dave!"

The other driver lowered his window, and they passed the time of day. The other driver lit a cigarette as he talked.

Diane wrinkled her nose as the smoke wafted by. "Does he really have to do that?" she muttered.

"Oh, come on," Adam said. "That can't possibly bother you from way over there. You converts are insufferable." He patted her knee with approval. He'd been delighted when she quit. Thank heaven she had finally seen the light, he'd said.

Light? Light had nothing whatever to do with it, though she didn't say so. A child someday was only a possibility, but if there was any chance at all, cigarettes had to go.

Suddenly she remembered something Charlie had said when they'd talked about smoking.

Kind of a deal. To appease Fate.

She must add it to her list. Perhaps Ed Ramirez would know what that had been about.